D E F R S ' U

A A B E H L P T

FREUD'S ALPHABET

JONATHAN TEL

Scribner

First published in Great Britain by Scribner, 2003
An imprint of Simon & Schuster UK Ltd
A Viacom Company

1 3 5 7 9 10 8 6 4 2

Simon & Schuster UK Ltd
Africa House
64–78 Kingsway
London WC2B 6AH

Simon & Schuster Australia
Sydney

www.simonsays.co.uk

A CIP catalogue record for this book is available from the British
Library

ISBN 0-7432-3916-4

Typeset by M Rules
Printed and bound in Great Britain by
The Bath Press, Bath

Picture credits: pp viii, 30, 134, 170 – Freud Museum, London;
pp 64, 100 – Imperial War Museum (negative numbers H7346 and
HU36137 respectively).

For Father, at last

'It was said in the name of Rabbi Bena'ah: "There were twenty-four dream interpreters in Jerusalem. Once I had a dream and consulted with every one of them. This one interpreted for me one thing, and that one another. And they all came true."'

Babylonian Talmud

Summer is far from over. It is going to be a beautiful day. In a northern suburb of London, at 20 Maresfield Gardens, a detached house of modest proportions lies empty and open to the world. Its front door is ajar, as are all the windows: the gazes of occasional passers-by are uninterrupted by leaded pane or net curtain even. But strangers do not linger since there is nothing yet to see. A sunbeam zeroes in on the Welcome mat. A clot of soot tumbles down the chimney. A distant air-raid siren blasts its warning – to be followed a minute later by the All Clear. But these are only for the sake of practice – as everyone should know.

Outside the house, a removal van is parked. Two removal men, one of a dark complexion and the other lighter, are manoeuvring a bulky object between them up a ramp and into the porch and thence the house. It is early: they are taking their time. They are chain-smoking Player's 'No Name': they leave a spoor of ash wherever they go. Item number one is a long dense beige cylinder – which, when set down on the living room floor and unrolled, proves to be a Persian carpet. In the course of the next hour or so, unrushed, they carry in a settee, a love seat, a sideboard veneered in bird's-eye maple, five non-matching chairs (one rocking), a ball of maroon wool, a box of Romeo y Julieta cigars, a secretaire, a bunch of silk flowers, two looking glasses (to be established facing one another almost but not quite parallel), portraits of ancestors and friends and a fearsome expressionist mountainscape, sixteen framed diplomas and certificates of membership in learned societies and honorary fellowships and awards in Latin, German, French, Swedish, Italian, Spanish, Dutch, and (in one case) English, a Notification of Registration of an Enemy Alien issued by the Metropolitan Police, a family-size bottle of morphine, a syringe, a silver toothpick, as well as circa three hundred pounds avoirdupois of papers and books – not necessarily in that order. Also several display cases containing a selection of Greek and Egyptian gods, and a host of exotic divinities besides. All the above the removal men arrange as best they can in the largest room on the ground floor.

They have brought no furnishings for the rest of the house (kitchen, say, or bathroom; let alone bedroom) since their van is not as capacious as it might be – they will have to make several more trips to the warehouse. Just as the dark man is about to climb into the driving seat, his comrade whistles an extract from a popular song of that period. The dark one replies in cockney rhyming slang. The long and the short of it is that they had almost forgotten one important object. Once more they unbar the back of the van: and what they carry out is best described as a couch. It is a magnificent specimen: oak-framed, stuffed with horsehair, and upholstered in studded pig's leather; design-wise it bears a strong affinity to the classic chaise longue with hints of the ottoman. How slowly and gracefully it is borne on the Englishmen's shoulders, across a portion of roadway, up over the kerb, and high above the pavement: one could imagine it is destined to drift forever through the peaceful suburb; a swallow swoops onto a seam, tugs out a single protruding horsehair, and flies away with it, in order to weave its find into a nest . . . Eventually however the couch arrives in the very heart of the room. Where it comes to earth. It is rotated so as to lie along the axis of the pair of looking glasses, for reflection's sake. It is draped with a Turkish rug. One of the legs, being a little too short, is propped up on *The Interpretation of Dreams*, a convenient hardback. The removal men retreat and disappear. The intertwined trail of ash stirs in the faintest breeze.

And in the shadows at the back of the room a man is waiting. He is stiff as a statue. He is facing the head of the couch. His name is . . . but his name is not the point. He is The Doktor. He is old. His suit, of Continental cut, is lavender-grey and his homburg is sepia which is a different kind of grey. His beard is white, but stained. His face, sadly, is yet another shade of grey. For cancer is eating him: his palate has already been destroyed, and replaced by a prosthesis made of gutta-percha and surgical quality steel.

This man believes in silence. Only by remaining silent, waiting for the other to speak first, can one hope to find out the truth.

He hopes and fears the silence he will find in London. Better, surely, than the noise in the Vienna he just came from.

At any rate he anticipates he will be privy to no conversations or analyses or jokes or stories here – since (though he has mastered several European tongues, and absorbed Shakespeare in the original) he can understand and utter spoken English only of the phrasebook variety. Yet, on the other hand, much can be communicated in an almost unknown language . . . He half-wishes he had ended up elsewhere, in a comprehensible place; but then, such thoughts are pointless – the fate that brought him here (as opposed to Paris or Amsterdam or Shanghai or Buenos Aires or Jerusalem or New York . . . where numbers of his friends and colleagues have settled . . . or a thousand other cities) is irreversible. He will conclude his days in no house, no city, no world other than this one. Yet he is free to envision, at least, the alternatives.

Silence persists.

It seems a question has been asked.

The Doktor shakes his head vigorously from side to side.

'*Ja ja*,' says the palatal prosthesis.

Apple

Midday. The streets of the suburb are a symphony of noise and bustle. Rumble of an iron wheel whipped by a boy along Netherhall Gardens. Giggle of three Belsize Lane girls playing blind man's buff. Whine of the portable pedal-powered machine which the knife grinder is utilizing for sharpening a pair of sewing scissors handed to him by the Irish kitchen maid at 18 Sumpter Close. (Will he succeed in enticing her to let him have a go on her cutlery? 'I must ask permission of my housekeeper,' she whispers.) Now here comes a clatter and clop as Hannibal, a piebald nag, drags a cart along Finchley Road; the rag-and-bone man's cry of 'Any old iron?' Click as two marbles (a clearie and a glassie), on Frognal Court, strike. Quintuple chink of a dropped six-pence bouncing twice on tarmacadam, thrice on the sewer grate; it plunges underneath Nutley Terrace. Modulated wheeze as a Spitfire (training mission) overflies the entire

5

neighourhood. Miscellaneous dog barks. Footfall. Bicycle hiss Car moan. Wind. Distant traffic noise rising and falling like the wind. Distant conversation likewise . . . And into this clamour, silence is leaking.

Silence is leaking. It emanates from an upper-storey room in a detached house in Maresfield Gardens. An old man is sitting there, on a straight-back chair in front of a desk by the shut window. He is in absolute silence. His right hand is resting on the desk. He is not wearing his spectacles: hence is gazing at no particular – relying, temporarily, on his sense of touch. He is gripping between finger and thumb a few (uncountably many; yet a few) brownish or greyish hairs. His right hand trembles.

The hairs are his wife's. His absent wife's. (Dead? As good as.) A hair he had found adhering to a watercolour brush; it had been her hobby. Several hairs that had clung to the chain of his own fob watch; he had come across them, quite unexpectedly, not long after the emigration. How, under what circumstances, her head had come into contact with the chain, he has no idea; yet it must have happened. Those hairs were among the greyer ones. As for the brown hairs, brown signifies lust. ('Let's see if a big boy, his veins pumping with rich blood, can catch hold of your tresses and unwind them!' he had written to her not long after their engagement.) Many of these he had surreptitiously harvested from between the prongs of her tortoiseshell comb, the bristles of her silver-backed brush. Now he opens the leather-bound photograph album, and turns it to a certain page. He fits on his glasses. Yes. Silence settles like fog. He rests the hairs on her photographed hair.

And in another room, elsewhere in this city, another old man is sitting, in silence, poring over an album, placing salvaged hairs on top of their image . . . And in yet a third room, and a fourth, and fifth, and many more, other men are echoing this fond act. For it is a given: that whatever is true of the first man, is true of mankind in this city, and surely indeed of all humanity.

(And even if a man were accompanied by his daughter, as it might be, or a wife, nevertheless he would be solitary – if only in that nobody else can feel one's pain, and each man's death is his alone.)

Certainly the first man is aware of his role. He understands his own significance. He rescues the hairs, and turns quickly to another page in the album. A group shot from the Great War: the sons in military uniform. Flick back to them as boys, on holiday at Berchtesgaden, dressed in Bavarian hats and jerkins and leather shorts. Little Anna about to bite a fruit. Sophie in the fashionable 'shroud' dress. He loves them. And in all these rooms, the old men are loving their children; their eyes are becoming damp; there is a jagged ache in the exact middle of their head. And the first man turns the page again, backwards. His father: he hates him. Once his father had told him an anecdote concerning his own youth in Moravia. A peasant had approached his father, then young, and had said, 'You dirty Jew, get out of my path!' and had slapped the fur hat off the father's head. And what had the father done? He had dodged out of the peasant's way, and had picked up his fur hat, dusted it down, and run off. Yes, the old man has no choice but to hate his father, to knock him down, to wish to kill him . . . And in all these rooms, in all the city, all men desire to kill the father . . . But, ah, what about the mother? (He turns the page again, back.) She is in the first blush of girlhood in this picture, a studio daguerreotype so reflective it is hard to view, she is wearing a satin dress, a pearl necklace, a broad 'conversation' hat her hair is leaking out of; he loves her; he wants to sleep with her. As all men do, in this city; as they must; since whatever is true of the first man, is always true. The album is closed. There is only silence here.

And there is only silence here. For there is nothing to be done. The mother and the father are dead; the wife, the children are absent; the man himself is dying. And if all the silences, if all the rooms, if all the ancient, thoughtful men were compiled together, they and their memories, their relics, their considerations, what would they add up to? A mother and a father, composite blurry images; a wife of equal vagueness; an erasure of children; an old man, an old man's silence . . . a great silence . . . and all the saved hairs would scarcely make up one lock.

Boy

Regent's Park. Early afternoon. A clear sky apart from a handful of clouds shaped like penny loaves. A nanny strolls along the sanded path, wheeling a vast navy-blue perambulator, with its hood up to protect from the elements a tiny, well-swaddled infant. Another nanny follows at a discreet distance. And then another. A fleet of perambulators, sailing off towards the horizon. These are followed by an old man in a Bath chair, being wheeled by a young girl, quite possibly his granddaughter. (An ironic inversion, yes; too pointed to seem altogether natural.) Then a boy in a sailor suit whipping a hoop. And another boy trying to whip a top – but of course the top won't spin properly on this gritty surface: it just falls over and dies. And a sailor, having difficulty in keeping his balance on dry land. A young woman of exceptional beauty, a blonde, walks by next, looking neither to right nor left. She is followed shortly by a brunette, equally beautiful. There is a pause, while the path is unoccupied.

The Doktor is seated on a wooden bench, admiring this scene, the parade of passers-by. It seems quite perfect; if anything a touch too perfect. Furthermore, it is compositionally incomplete.

He is contrasting the city he happens to be in with the city which is, for him, the obverse of this one – Paris. It was there that he went in his youth, free from his family. There that he experienced extraordinary pleasures of the flesh and of the mind. There that he studied Medicine and Psychology under his *maître*, the great Dr Charcot. Ah, what a delight to work hard by day, and in the evening to take on the role of a *flâneur*, to gather with one's friends in a café and engage in passionate philosophical conversation, whilst smoking a cigar. He prided himself on his flawless accent and his remarkable command of the idiomatic tongue. He seriously dreamed of staying on and turning into a Parisian himself – back in those years before his country stumbled into war with France . . . He grunts.

What is pressing into his back is a brass plaque affixed to the slats of the bench:

IN MEMORY MARY CHAFFINCH-WILSON (1863–1931)
'A GARDEN IS A LOVESOME THING, GOD WOT'

But what would the authorities have done if Mary Chaffinch-Wilson had not cared for this particular place? Would there have been no bench? Would there have been a bench elsewhere, in a beauty spot she preferred? Would this bench have existed anyway, but been dedicated to someone else, or to nobody? And the same goes for the fragment of verse. It states that gardens are lovely. Well, yes. But wouldn't they have been just as lovely without the poem? Possibly, in this city, not.

As he sits there, a gardener passes nearby, dragging a lawnmower. The handle rests in front of the gardener's chest: he might as well be yoked to it. The rotary blade turns, chopping the grass into short segments. This lawnmower is the kind that has no box behind it to catch the leavings – instead the green stuff is forced out, splattering all over The Doktor.

As he only now notices: the gardener is female (so many males have been called up into the armed forces) – a staggeringly beautiful redhead (why yes! just what was needed to constitute the complete set). She is floating away in front of her machine, suffusing a green mist – Titania on her chariot.

She turns and comes back! Now she is gliding towards him. Once more she passes him, quite close; he is enveloped in the miasma of minced grass. The bits of vegetable matter settle on his knees and *where* to the woollen material of his Continental-cut three-piece; *several* cling to the crown of his homburg.

And a third time she lofts past: a third *time* he is caught up in her viridescence: a third time he experienc*es* an erotic and intellectual satisfaction. A third time she goes aw*ay* – now, however, never to return.

The Doktor sniffs. The sweet aroma of freshly cut grass. Aha! he is beginning to have an inkling: he is spotting the deliberate mistake. For the grass smells 'sweet' and that is it. The subtle, the infinitely complex aroma that this would have elsewhere, that it did have, to his certain knowledge, in Paris, is absent in this city.

And this does not just apply to the grass. He sniffs quite hard. The odours of roses, of traffic . . . all simplified, flattened out, reducible to one or at most a pair of adjectives.

(For a moment, scared, he wonders if this signifies a defect in him. But no, of course not, it is in the nature of the place.)

Similarly the women here are 'beautiful' – or 'ugly' – or 'plain' – but the vast range of intermediate and intricate kinds of female beauty, the kinds he had known in earlier years, is lacking here. Adults in general belong to some definable profession, which is indicated in an emblematic manner – the butcher's boy is carrying a side of beef; the wet nurse clutches a baby to her bosom; the barrister wears his wig in public; the candlestick maker just happens to have a specimen of her craft in her satchel. Only richer men and younger women are permitted not to bother with a job – and they are usually, ostentatiously in love. Ah, passionate lovers abound – sometimes they permit themselves the coyest of fluttering kisses; on other occasions their behaviour is positively pornographic: there are no gradations in between.

To verify his hypothesis he reaches behind himself and strokes – for want of better – a tree trunk. He pinches it; he caresses it. A ginkgo, an old one. The bark is 'rough' where it is scarred; other parts are 'smooth' – everything that is writable in words about bark texture is writable about this bark (one could devote paragraphs to an enumeration of its wrinkliness, its scuffed scratchy patches, its damp adherence) but the textural complexity one would expect in nature, that one is entitled to expect, the innumerable kinds and attributes of natural texture that no words can capture, that are beyond words, that words only get in the way of understanding, are missing here.

For this city has been put too much into words. It has been novelized – it has also been short-storified; poets and essayists too have done their bit to chip away at it – yes, the novelists above all, by rubbing away at it so often and so hard, have eroded the details. They have smoothed it down into the shapes permitted by the English language. This city is no more nor less than its fictional equivalent.

Were an Eskimo, with his supposed hundred words for snow, to come here in midwinter – he would find no use for ninety-nine of them. An Arabian girl playing in the sandbox in the Hampstead Heath playground, she would be able to use but one out of the score of sand words that she knows. This city has been so moulded by its fictional descriptions that even another language could not rescue it.

At least this city has been granted narrative structure: a series of incidents selected on some arbitrary-seeming basis are sure to arrange themselves to tell a story (much as the biography of anybody, no matter how chaotic the life, will always have a beginning, a middle and an end).

The Doktor eavesdrops. On the neighbouring bench a conversation is taking place between four youngish people, two seated and two standing, of both sexes. Although he cannot actually comprehend it (it is too rapid; too idiomatic), he can get the rhythm of it, the development. First a tenor is uttering a soliloquy; which is succeeded by a brief soprano interlude; then a baritone and a contralto declare alternate phrases; finally the tenor, on his own, reprises his contribution, concluding on a dying note. But what is noteworthy is that every snatch of dialogue is coherent (quite unlike that in other cities he could name); hardly anybody ever interrupts and when this is unavoidable, a brief yelp or cry of, 'No!' is considered quite sufficient; under no circumstances will two or more people emit well-formed strands of speech simultaneously. That this is novel-format speech is incontrovertible – the quality and genre is quite another question.

The Doktor decides to investigate this phenomenon in more detail. He rises with care from the bench, and grips his walking stick in his pigskin-gloved hand. Slowly he advances down the path towards Euston. He veers off across the meadow and peers behind the bushes. An assortment of absences: whatever is indescribable is non-existent.

As The Doktor turns and heads back towards his home, he ponders this strange city. In many ways it is horrible: a painter would chafe at its limitations; a revolutionary would be frustrated; a sensualist would have to emigrate; but when it comes to his own business . . . ah well, it seems the novelists have not done such a bad job: the range of personalities, of characters, of thoughts, of psychological complexes, is so vast as to pass for unlimited.

Cat

Walking down Fitzjohn's Avenue in the course of his daily constitutional, The Doktor observes a peculiar phenomenon. A woman in her middle years, wearing an apron specked with raspberry jam and smeared with comma-shaped egg stains, is crouching near the servants' entrance of a mock-Tudor villa. Not far away, scurrying between the substantial iron dustbins, is a mongrel with much terrier in it. The woman claps her hands. A cloud of flour arises. 'Come here, Mother-in-law!' she calls. The dog comes bounding towards her. She welcomes it by ruffling its scruffy nape. Next she yells, 'Fido! come!' This time it is a cat, a tabby stalking along the porch parapet, that plummets into the grinning woman's lap. She feeds a slice of jam tart to each of her carnivorous pets. This city, then, must be a place where everything is called by the inexact name and treated inappropriately. But why? What purpose might this serve? The logic of it escapes The Doktor.

But soon – while waiting for the traffic lights at the inter-section with Adelaide Road – he is confronted with a comparable instance. Progressing in a direction perpen-dicular to his, a man and a woman, not so young, arm in arm, go by. He deduces they must be lovers, on the basis of their synchronized strut, and from their habit of winking and pouting at one another. Interestingly, however, pinned to the somewhat baggy seat of the man's tweed plus fours is a scrap of paper inscribed in blue ink with the motto KICK ME. The man surely is unaware of this. Yet the woman could hardly avoid noticing it; indeed the conclusion is inescapable that she attached it there. This must constitute, on her part, a 'joke'.

The Doktor is most fascinated by jokes, though he seldom laughs at them. Indeed, he has written a whole book of the utmost seriousness on this very subject. Jokes, he holds, are constructed like dreams; and dreams like jokes. He considers jocularity to be a deviant activity rooted in the psychopathology of the unconscious mind. Now at last, he realizes, he is living in a city where joking is compulsory. Where strong emotions can only be expressed slantwise. Where even the most casual greeting is obliged to be a pun or a jeer. Where everyone is addressed by a deliberately inapt nickname (short folk are known as Lofty; the tall as Titch) or a gibing insult, 'Him with the beetroot complexion', 'Big Foot'. Where even The Doktor himself is chuckled at each morning by the postman 'Hullo, Doctor Fraud!'

And this saddens The Doktor. For he well knows that joking is a form of aggression, directed against the other, and, masochistically, the self.

Imagine a city composed out of quips. What would it be like? The roads would wind mazily and peter out in subtle dead ends, or be blocked by trenches wherein air-raid shelters are being constructed. Barrage balloons, giant silvery heffalumps, would be tethered over Regent's Park, and wobble. Should one wait for a bus (the number 13 to Piccadilly Circus, say) for a full forty minutes none would arrive, and then half a dozen, a pride of buses, would all come trundling along together. The very houses would be constructed in pastiche styles – mock this, revival that, imitation the other, and furnished inside with kitschy *objets d'art*: Caravaggio place mats; vases in the form of lascivious negresses; a chaise longue on ball-claw feet; an electric light switch angled like a nose (retroussé means off; hook: on); ostentatiously etiolated salt cellars and pepper mills . . . all for the sake of worshipping the great god Humour.

The public buildings, likewise. Cinema and *palais de danse*, church and hospital, present a pseudo Assyrian or Egyptian face to the world, or Chinoiserie; a certain synagogue's façade resembles the front portion of a Rolls Royce.

The cuisine is a notorious joke. Breakfast might consist of a slice of fried bread and half a boiled tomato. Coffee is paler than tea: tea is stewed to the point of bitterness and doused with milk. As for lunch and supper . . . but let us not speak of lunch and supper.

In the Cosmo restaurant on Finchley Road, at tea time, The Doktor orders the famous sherry trifle. It is supposed to consist of a base of fluffy sponge cake inspired with alcohol, topped with cream and custard and fruit; but the chef has been too lavish with the bottle. The Doktor is presented with a kind of fruit punch – a bowl of amontillado speckled with edible flotsam.

And it is not just a question of externalities. In this city it is held that jokiness is essential: it is in the nature of thought and of fate. Recruits on basic training, exercising in preparation for the coming War, come charging out of the hydrangeas in Queen Mary's Flower Garden, Regent's Park. An ex Trichinopoly boxwallah in the Hospital for Tropical Diseases, about to pass away from yellow fever complicated with tertiary syphilis, cracks pathetic puns for the benefit of his phantom chums ('How did you find your steak, sir?' 'I looked under the lettuce, and there it was!' 'Waiter! What kind of soup is this?' 'It's bean soup, sir.' 'I don't care what it's been, what kind of soup is it now!?') as he is served, intravenously, his last meal.

And the art confirms this. The poetry here is ironic. The audience at every play, no matter how tragic, finds occasion to titter. As for literature, members of the bourgeoisie take pleasure in reading about people just like themselves being found slumped in the library, a dagger of oriental design plunged between the shoulder blades. And when it comes to music . . . but of course there is no decent music.

And love. At 11 Nutley Terrace, Mr and Mrs M—, a long-married couple who hate one another, who sleep in separate bedrooms, who pursue parallel lives for the most part, happen to arrive simultaneously in the bathroom, each eager to use it. There is no other bathroom on the premises. Mr M— remarks, 'How delightful to see you.' His wife responds, 'And you, too.' The husband adds, 'We must get together more often.' She replies, 'We can't go on meeting like this.' Conversely, in the canteen of the Royal Zoological Society, a female reptile superintendent carries her tray of half-past-threeses (steaming cocoa, iced bun) over to the table where a male elephant washer is already seated. He has long lusted after her. 'Do you mind awfully?' she says. He answers, 'There's no law against it, is there?'

Indeed, it is clear that the inhabitants of this city do not like their jokes. They deplore them. They wish, for once, they could talk and behave unjokily about something. But what can they do? Life is one big joke. Just possibly the forthcoming War (or so savants dream) might grant a brief opportunity for seriousness.

It is time for The Doktor to hasten home. He waves and yells, 'Taxi!' to the empty road.

And when he arrives in his consulting room, the patient is already on the couch. His name is Maurice R—. He is a portly fellow, wearing a chalkstriped three-piece in dark blue wool. He is the manager and owner of a profitable textiles factory a few miles to the north, in the vicinity of Golders Green. For forty years he was married, blissfully, to Bessie R— (née S—). Recently she died. It is his savage grief that has caused him to seek The Doktor's help.

As Maurice R— tells of his tragedy, his anguish, he does it in such a wry deadpan manner that The Doktor himself can scarcely suppress a snigger.

Diamond

Tap-tapping his siver-ferruled bamboo walking stick (gift from a grateful princess) like a blind man, he makes his way out of the dim bedroom and along the upper-floor corridor, and stands at the end of it, looking out through the little leaded window – a square of brightness subdivided into four component squares. He sees the scuffed yellow-green of the lawn below, and the two trees at the end of his property (poplar, cherry), and through a gap between the different kinds of foliage, and through a corresponding gap between the chimneys on a pair of farther houses, he can peruse a tiny fraction of Finchley Road. A busy highway. Where pedestrians hustle past, and buses, and lorries, cars of course, even the occasional horse-drawn cart. There is a crack in one of the panes; light catches there – a golden scar across London.

*

The Doktor remembers the conflagration that destroyed the Crystal Palace. He saw it with his own eyes, in silent monochrome on the newsreel in the faded gilt luxury of the Orpheum Bioskop on Ringstrasse in Vienna; the Wurlitzer uttered plangent variations on themes from *Götterdämmerung*; it was followed by a Charlie Chaplin double feature.

The Crystal Palace was born in the same decade as The Doktor. It appeared in 1851 – a futuristic emblem of steel and glass – established within Hyde Park in the centre of London. The construction was so vast that whole trees (a triad of venerable elms) remained *in situ* while the Palace rose about them. It housed the Great Exhibition of the Arts and Manufactures of All Nations. Which presented the finest attainments of that era – the Hydraulic Press, the Combine Harvester, the Unpickable Lock, the Fruit Flavoured Jelly, the Malachite Throne Room of the Tsar of All The Russias . . . As you entered (and almost anybody could afford to, struggle if you must, on a Shilling Day, at least) the first image to greet your eyes would be the Captive Slave, by the American sculptor Hiram Power – a nude lady of a pleasing plumpness, in marble, shackled, her eyes delicately averted. How The Doktor wishes he had been there, at around the time of his own conception, to see and take part.

After the Exhibition was over, the Palace was dismantled – and reconstructed in rather different form on open
ground in a London suburb lying about as far south from the
Thames as The Doktor is to the north. Where it was used as
a locale for various temporary expositions . . . circus . . . pan-
tomime . . . pedigree dog show . . . Buffalo Bill . . .

In 1936 it burnt down. It had been fabulously flammable
(this was stated after the event): a miracle it had survived so
long! The luminosity of it (the great chandelier teardrops of
molten glass, the glowing bars of white-hot steel) that the
whirring projector had blazed on the great screen of the
Orpheum – surely this was the apotheosis of the Palace, the
longed-for culmination.

The Doktor mutters to himself a quote from Shakespeare
(in Schiller's superb translation): 'I could not wish the act
undone, the issue of it being so proper' – as Gloucester says
in *King Lear*, referring to the conception of his bastard son
Edmund (who will shortly thereafter yawn in the wings
while the old man's eyes are being plucked out).

He imagines the Palace presenting itself as a prospective
patient. He would have it stretch itself out on his couch. He
would explain the hidden motivation underlying its self-
destructiveness, elucidate the dream-clues; or rather, he
would have the Palace come to realize this for itself (himself?
herself? – surely both he and she at once and together!)

The death-wish, yes. For the desire for oblivion underlies this city. The proof rests in dreams. Consider: what do dreams do? They recur. And what does recurrence signify? The need to go back: back to childhood: to birth: to the time before birth: the time when one does not exist.

The Doktor blinks. He realizes now why thoughts of the Crystal Palace had flickered and raged in his head. For he is seeing an omnibus, a hefty red double-decker, stuck in the traffic along Finchley Road, temporarily. The number of the bus is 2. Let this bus be not the 2A (which goes no farther than the heart of London) but its rival and alter ego: a bus whose forehead is marked, Cain-wise, with the following number and letter and destination: 2B – CRYSTAL PALACE.

Of course it cannot literally go to the Palace – since time runs in only one direction; at best this bus could transport one to the site of it, in the south. Nothing to behold there, now.

Yet, with all due seriousness, The Doktor considers taking this bus. He would walk as far as the stop, near the Underground station. He would wave his hand to flag it down, or possibly his stick. He would be helped on board. He would arrange himself on a padded seat, by a window. He would pay his fare (fivepence halfpenny). The bus would glide and shudder past the cake shop which is to be demolished by a V-2 in five years' time, past Lord's Cricket

Ground, past a cemetery, past the row of brothels that existed a century previously, past the great golden dome and minaret of the Mosque that will, thanks to Saudi oil money, be built forty years in the future, past 221B Baker Street and Madame Tussaud's, past the Marble Arch that commemorates a war triumph against Napoleon, past Victoria Station, and (heading ever south) via a bridge across the Thames, transit through dank slums to districts each one clearer and lighter than the previous, arriving ultimately at where the Crystal Palace had stood for many decades, for the best part of The Doktor's life – a park-invested suburb similar to the one he is living in now.

No, there would be no point in making this journey. And yet . . .

A momentary flash of light stabbing, it feels, from jaw to palate to medulla oblongata to the crown of the head.

The traffic blockage eases; the 2B swerves off, its upper storey swaying like a howdah on an elephant. No matter: for were he to make his way to the stop, another bus with the same destination would come along soon enough.

He is still undecided . . .

. . . 2B or not . . .

. . . or take up arms against a sea of troubles, and, by opposing, end them.

Elephant

That War will break out soon, though denied by some, is evident. The Doktor's fear and hope is not his alone: this is the condition of the city, the country, the world. A platoon of fresh recruits, under the tutelage of an ex India Army sergeant major, is marching through the northern suburbs of London. The volunteers assembled outside the Underground station at Golders Green; thence they scrambled across the Heath to Hampstead, and now they are heading via the High Street, and Belsize Grove, and Primrose Hill Road, in the direction of the Regent's Park zoo.

As they march along, they chant

We're here because
We're here because
We're here because
We're here because . . .

From time to time the sergeant major bawls instructions. 'Atten-shun! At-tease! Presen-tarms! Lef-ri! Lef-ri! Lef-ri!' The privates do their best to obey.

The sergeant major's voice becomes more and more distorted. Eventually only the rhythm and the pitch of his words remain – yet this is sufficient to communicate – like the beat of the talking drums used by the Yoruba of Western Africa.

The army is taking a short cut down Eton Avenue and Strathray Gardens and Lancaster Grove and Buckland Crescent and Maresfield Gardens . . . the hypothesis that it has become lost is getting more probable.

Drawn by the noise, The Doktor stands by the unopenable jammed window in his upper floor bedroom, his nose pressed against the pane. What he observes is a not unexpected sight – that which he must have recurrently envisioned – a group of men in civilian clothing (for their uniforms have not yet been issued) shuffling along in step and carrying, to serve as a dummy weapon, some long thinnish object. Each man is in his own dream: collectively they are in The Doktor's. The chimney sweep bears his brush with pride. The butcher his cleaver. The baker his loaf. The office clerk his umbrella, for want of better. The sixth-former his cricket bat. The banker a roll of financial statements, secured with a red ribbon. The bartender erects a pint bottle of Bass Pale Ale.

The Doktor raises his right hand in a proud salute – a general reviewing his troops.

'Are you in pain?' Jones says.

The Doktor does not answer. His beard shivers in the breeze. It is a hot August afternoon, and The Doktor, formal in thickly striped dark suit and stiff hat, hunches on the grass with his hands encircling his shins. Jones, wearing navy blue bathing trunks, is cross-legged alongside.

They have made it as far as the lawn that leads down to the Men's Pond on Hampstead Heath. Figures dive and splash, sending up glitter. Since everybody here is male, some permit themselves undress; others are in a variety of more or less revelatory costumes. A team of zestful civil servants in Union Jack leotards perform callisthenics on the far side of the pond: they leap with legs together and arms by the side, while shouting in unison, 'Cup!' – then 'Saucer!' – they bound again with limbs extended. Out of nowhere a naked lithe white-haired fellow runs dodging between the civil servants up to the pool's brink, jumps, tucks himself into a somersault, and uncurls into the water. A drop splatters on The Doktor's thumb-knuckle; he appears to be intent on observing the process of its evaporation and drip.

'Are you in pain still?' Jones has brought his black bag with him; he gestures vaguely at it. He is acting as personal physician to The Doktor, among his other capacities. 'I could give you a tenth of a grain of morphia, hmm? I think that would do the trick.'

The Doktor opens his mouth. He is talking about his sojourn in this city. But what with his palatal awkwardness, his speech is difficult to understand. Even Jones, who is The Doktor's official translator (his ambition is to English the best part of the *Gesammelte Werke*: the Complete Works), can catch no more than the odd word.

'What's that?' says Jones. 'Just how many months ago are we talking about? Where? Which summer? Which year?'

The Doktor continues describing his explorations of the city, his successive attempts to understand it, one way or another.

'Come, come. Are you seriously stating you have ventured out into the city, unaccompanied?'

And now The Doktor appears to be mentioning some of his recent patients, his case studies.

Jones says, 'But . . . that's scarcely . . . and in which language? . . . not in your condition. Surely you jest?'

Three boys in tennis clothes skip arm in arm down the grassy slope and straight into the water. Laughing, they splutter and choke and gasp; their rackets float off towards the deep end.

Several vicars are picking daisies and assembling them in a chain.

A plump middle-aged man sunbathes on a puce towel laid precisely parallel to the diving board. He is nude. A red hardback, one of the publications of the Left Book Club, is balanced on his paunch. He dog-ears relevant pages.

An air-raid siren whines. Nobody pays it any particular attention. Surely it is yet another practice, or a false alarm. The warning is to be heeded by factory workers and shoppers, schoolchildren and nursing mothers – they will all duly huddle under the Morrison shelter in the drawing room; or rush out into the back garden Anderson shelter; or descend into the well-sandbagged basement. But one can hardly expect swimmers and nature worshippers to take its threat seriously; the thought that a bomb might explode while one is performing the breaststroke or sprawling semi-clothed on a lawn – that is absurd: it is beyond belief.

Only the fat socialist nudist has put on a gas mask. He turns, the better to apply an equitable degree of tan to his rear.

The siren fades. Its echo – no, its after-sound – persists.

Silence, of a sort.

(Shrieks of jollity; splashings; distant birdsong . . . these are of no account.)

There is no All Clear yet.

This absence appears to be a sufficient signal. The Doktor unlaces his half-brogues. He removes shoes and socks, the layers of his suit and of his knitted combinations, and arranges them on the ground – in the shape of a scrawny, flattened Invisible Man. He lifts off his hat, and sets it on the grass, an appropriate distance above the collar. Finally he doffs his spectacles, folds their wings, and places these down also. Now he is naked (except, of course, that a bearded man can never be absolutely undressed). He struggles to his feet. How painfully pale The Doktor looks, how bony, how foreign.

Jones jumps up. He strides after The Doktor, who is tottering down the slope.

'Are you sure that is altogether advisable?' Jones calls.

But it is too late. The Doktor has already jumped. He is underwater . . .

. . . his hair quivers like seaweed . . . then he cannot be seen . . .

. . . and he surfaces, several yards away, puffing and waving.

Jones dives in.

When Jones surfaces, The Doktor is not at first in view – but there he is! – surprisingly far out, floating on his front. Jones swims after.

The Doktor is progressing across the pond in a steady dog paddle. Jones, by dint of his powerful breaststroke, pursues and overtakes him. Thereupon the two psychoanalysts: the master and the disciple, the foreigner and the native, the naked and the partly clothed, the dying and the not-yet-dying, swim side by side towards the deep end . . .

. . . when suddenly, while at the very middle of the pool, out of The Doktor's mouth emerges a small mobile object. It is the palatal prosthesis. It bobs on the gentle waves; the gutta-percha portion swings on stainless steel hinges; as if the thing were blabbing to itself.

Jones treads water.

The Doktor keeps dog-paddling.

The prosthesis is advancing in a reasonably energetic freestyle.

The Doktor does not increase his pace (presumably he lacks the athletic skill) but nor does he slacken. His persistence enables him to close the gap somewhat.

The prosthesis surges ahead. It wriggles and chatters.

The Doktor (slow but steady) is catching up again.

It appears to be a pretty evenly matched contest. The prosthesis quick but erratic; The Doktor physically weak but determined. Jones, ever tactful, watches from a discreet distance; besides, his sense of fair play would forbid him to interfere. The other swimmers in the pond, they too move aside to let this old man deal with his own problem. It seems after all The Doktor will not overtake the prosthesis, but nor will the latter escape utterly – neither side destined for a clear win.

But then, just as the competitors are approaching the pond's far edge, by means of a sharp hard arm-thrash and ankle-flap (his face twists in a shark-grin – an anguished grimace; his entire body shudders) The Doktor propels himself onward fast. He opens his mouth wide: he shuts it. Once again the prosthesis is contained within The Doktor.

France

It is well known that natives of different countries cannot make head nor tail of one another. True, they can commit themselves to attending lectures on foreign culture; they can take courses at the Berlitz School; they can read each other in translation; yet the essence is always missing. A Frenchman will never truly understand a German; nor a Greek a Turk; a Pole a Czech. Even within one country much the same is valid. What goes on in the head of a Liverpudlian will never be known by a citizen of Manchester; what is common knowledge in Bath is, in Bournemouth, gibberish.

And even within the one city, likewise. Inhabitants of the various districts and suburbs of London are renowned for misunderstanding and/or despising one another's view. 'Oh how Cricklewood!' is liable to be declared, scornfully. 'What a typically Twickenham remark!' 'Gosh how awfully

Wimbledon of you!' And these constitute fair comment. The separate languages, dialects, call them what you will, are sufficiently different as to debar proper mutual comprehension. Yet communication is not absolutely impossible. For multilingualism is a reality. (And this should not be confused with translatability. There are certain Swiss, for example, brought up at the intersections of linguistic boundaries, who couldn't translate so much as *Frère Jacques* to save their lives yet nevertheless speak fluently three or even four languages, and can think as many contradictory thoughts simultaneously.) Those Londoners who have lived or worked in different regions of the capital, and have a knack for the dialects, may take on the role of dragoman. They are often found in such capacities as door-to-door salesman, Justice of the Peace, ticket seller on the Underground. But these are the exceptions that prove the rule.

And it is not just a question of 'language' in the narrow sense. The same behaviour would have radically different significance depending on where it is carried out. A Stamford Hill boy who succeeds in becoming a professional boxer might be hailed as a hero; the same feat, if accomplished in Highgate, would be a matter for shame. A Bayswaterian who lies down weekly on a psychoanalyst's couch might boast about it with impunity; yet a hundred yards to the north across the Paddington frontier, it would be a dark secret.

The Doktor's own neighbourhood is an extreme example. For it has no clear definition. Maresfield Gardens lies, for political purposes, within the boundaries of the Borough of Hampstead; yet the residents would seldom define themselves thus. Some prefer to say they live in the sub-district known as Belsize Park. Others claim to belong to Swiss Cottage (so named after a restaurant-cum-pub, in mock-chalet style, erected nearby). Several characterize themselves as, 'I live near Finchley Road,' merely. Still others claim to inhabit Child's Hill – a quarter whose existence is known only to a select few. The estate agents have taken to describing the locality as South Hampstead. The upshot is that even close neighbours, who have lived next door all their lives, may think of themselves as residents of quite different districts, and treat each other with mutual disdain and puzzlement.

Yet there is a positive side to this Balkanization of the city. Since nobody can be sure of a genial reception outside the immediate surroundings, he or she will tend to stay put, and local customs develop. For example a Hampstead green-grocer's might sell swedes, while (a mere mile away) the Golders Green branch of the same establishment will stock turnips instead. The fat pale plums of Primrose Hill are quite unlike the thin dark ones obtainable across the border in Camden. Kentish Town's stationery shop offers just silvery drawing pins – in contrast to the coppery ones which are *de rigueur* in Gospel Oak. Nobody who feels at home in the pubs of Notting Hill would ever enjoy a pint in a Kilburn pub, or vice versa. When the bell rings for morning break, children in the playgrounds of Fitzrovia amuse themselves with 'Knock, knock' puns: the boys and girls of Soho find these not the least bit funny.

Naturally, then, most Londoners spend their lives in their own neighbourhood. The idea of visiting another is mildly comic; of relocating, unthinkable. Since they have never in fact ventured out seriously, they cannot know whether, in fact, they would be a fish out of water elsewhere; this is not an experiment they are willing to perform.

Yet there are exceptions. There are travellers who roam the city, from borough to borough, quarter to quarter, sampling the distinct quality of each: this one's hygienic cheese shop; that one's air of faded gentility; this one's amusing Great War memorial; that one's 'chirpy' quality . . . not quite comprehending any, but relishing the very lack of comprehension. And once one has left one's native suburb, one is condemned to keep moving endlessly: one will feel at home nowhere.

And what if one is a Doktor, seeking to present a theory

of universal applicability, which one cannot get across to these baffled and baffling foreigners? One will always, in all one's dealings with them, even when accepting a loaf from the baker's boy or asking the bus conductor for change, speak nothing but High German, loudly.

Gschnas

Suppose there is a city where just about everybody is jaunting about in aeroplanes. Goggles are all the rage, goggles and a heavy leather flying suit. One lives in a propeller 'plane and buzzes round and round. Occasionally of course, one would have to come to earth – to take a bath; to borrow a new Agatha Christie from the lending library; to refuel; to purchase a loaf of brown bread and a pot of bloater paste for one's tea . . . But soon, as soon as possible, one would taxi down the runway, pull back the joystick, and leap once more into the empyrean. One would be able to think of oneself as 'one' – superior and abstract. Ah, how pleasant to be home, home again, home in the sky.

Others, of a more old-fashioned disposition, prefer to inhabit dirigibles – substantial cigar-shaped craft that move as fast as the shadows of clouds, as slow as clouds, as slow as the shadows of people, as fast as diatoms in a drop of pond water. In no great hurry to go anywhere, the blimps circle the city in a holding pattern, sometimes moving in a figure-of-eight for reasons of aesthetic preference. Still other citizens, whose temperament is positively antique, bob about in hot-air balloons – veritable montgolfiers – decorated with classical motifs in the Deuxième Empire style.

And this by no means exhausts the possibilities. We are free to imagine various kinds of futuristic craft – shaped like spirals, or saucers, or arrows . . . fantastic sky-vehicles resembling winged galleons. Each inhabitant of the airscape to his or her own taste.

Could such a city really exist? It seems so. For, in the course of the last decade, a slew of artists, writers, thinkers, cartoonists . . . have been painting, describing, dreaming up, caricaturing this aerial lifestyle. It is commonly supposed to be a City of the Future – a projection of our present world up into one or another of the conceivable worlds-to-come. Let us presume, for the sake of argument then, it exists.

It exists! Even as we stroll down Primrose Hill Road clutching shopping bags filled with a week's supply of miscellaneous groceries, the twenty-pound bag of russet potatoes dragging us back; even as we toss an old tennis ball ahead of a bounding collie, 'Ethelred! Bring!'; even as the soles of our shoes press down, and down again, and down on an oblong granite paving stone, on clay marl, on coconut fibre flooring material, earthbound as we are, we can look up and see aircraft and airmen buzzing and whizzing overhead – the Royal Air Force at the ready – pilots from Hendon aerodrome tucked into the cockpits of Spitfires, getting in their flying practice; Sopwith Camels bluebottle-black against the sun; the new Lancasters performing dummy bombing runs over Regent's Park zoo; squadrons in formation setting out for their freshly laid-out bases in strategic locations – as far away as Northolt in the Midlands, as easterly as Saffron Walden . . . flying as high as, higher than, the Tower of Babel. And we know that if there is to be a battle for this city, it will be fought here: in the sky (for we have seen the newsreels from the Continent: we know that air power means everything). So we are assured that the lives of those superior young men in their aeroplanes are lived more intensely than our lives, and what they do is infinitely more important than anything we do, and that they never will descend from the sky until they are dead or absolute victory is won (or if they should, if they do, it shouldn't, it doesn't, really count). And our own lives are irrelevant by comparison. And if, statistically, only a tiny fraction of the population is skyborne – then to hell with statistics! We live in the air!

May our myths protect us!

In order to defend the city, barrage balloons have been tethered in the open spaces – on Hampstead Heath and

Regent's Park, Green Park and Hyde Park, Epping Forest and Clapham Common. The theory is that these large, soft, cartoony-looking vaguenesses will hinder the passage of enemy aircraft. And though they will prove ineffective yet we will never lose faith in them. They are stabilized with fins shaped, approximately, like Bugs Bunny's ears; like Dumbo's; like the Sphinx's breasts. And they are inhabited by squatters . . .

(Yes: this is an urban myth. And therefore undeniable.)

. . . loners, tramps, Conscientious Objectors who have clambered via the mooring cables to the yielding surface of the balloons themselves and built eyries high up there, home-from-homes, where they reside, overlooking the city, determined not to creep down again until there is no danger they will be conscripted. It is said that even some families have moved up to the balloons: Mum soaping and scrubbing the laundry against the washboard; Dad boiling up a pot of tea on the primus stove; Baby whimpering. If you peer with your eyes squinted, up there, up to the rim of the balloon where it cuts into the sun, you can see the tethering rope, and on it, the silhouettes of damp nappies hung out to dry, wafting like flags.

Truly this myth is told. This (truly) myth is told. This myth, truly, is told. This myth is truly told. This myth is told, truly.

The patient, Eloise G——, is supine on the Turkish rug which is spread on the couch. She is depressed. She is unsatisfied with her mundane life – though, objectively, it might seem fulfilling enough. A husband whom she loves and who loves her; children; an interesting job. She is nestled on the polychrome rug – its knotted pattern like an array of parks and canals, rows of shops and blocks of urban streets, viewed from on high. Her hands are angled out into space. Her fingertips extend.

'Sexual intercourse,' she is confessing. 'I dream about it. Every night I dream about nothing but sexual intercourse.'

The Doktor elucidates: 'To dream of sex signifies – the unconscious desire to fly.'

Hamlet

The postman is going on his early morning rounds. He leans his bicycle against the gate of number 7 Kidderpore Avenue, and carries his important bag up the slate path to the porch and front door. He pushes a delivery through the slot. What lands within, on the mat, is an electricity bill, a love letter, a misdirected Jewish New Year greeting, an unsolicited proposal from a life insurance company, a saucy seaside Wish You Were Here card, a bank statement. The inhabitants of number 7 pick up the post. The post is what exists: the man who brought it, as far as they are concerned, is neither here nor there.

What else might be said about this postman? He wears an appropriate uniform. His eyes are blue. He is a martyr to intermittent hiccoughs. His wife is pregnant with what will become the goalkeeper of a first-division football team 1962–67. He is a smell, a concatenation of alien smells, from the point of view of the corgi that claims number 7 as its territory and attempts to bite the postman's shin. He kicks out, hard, and misses.

But all these attempts at description are no more than what they are. They do not get at the essence of the man: for there is no essence or, if there is, it cannot be understood. You might as well expect the man's name ('Bob MacNeice' as it so happens) to reveal the secret of his identity; that would be like supposing that the title of a novel chapter should sum up the contents, rather than simply allude to them. This is a city without ego: where a person is knowable only in terms of his or her role.

A man in the second-hand heavy goods vehicle business is performing his goodbyes on the doorstep of a Sumatra Road maisonette. He is kissing. She is being kissed. She is his kept woman. He hands her several banknotes plus the loose change in his wallet. She counts it. Eighteen pounds eleven shillings and sixpence three farthings. She asks for more. He refuses: 'Do you think I'm made of money?' But he is: he consists of money and nothing but – for all that she cares.

The butcher, likewise, from the point of view of his customers, is a bagful of steaks and chops and sausages and offal and dog meat.

The florist is a bouquet of gladioli and roses and dahlias and carnations.

The rat-catcher is defined in terms of dead rodents.

The bellringer is a repeated chime.

The fiancée and fiancé kissing on Primrose Hill: they are a heaving bosom and a dowry, a finely formed backside with a sound career ahead, respectively.

But surely a single person may exist in many versions – wife, daughter, adultress, mother, supporting peasant in the South Hampstead Amateur Dramatic Society production of *St Joan*? Yet these serve only to multiply her, not to redefine her as a more complex somebody. For this city is not a predicate, a proposition from which some profundity might be deduced. It just is.

And what is oddest: the citizens make no attempt to slough off the stereotypes: to declare, 'This is the real me.' Either they are content with ignorance; or knowledge is what they fear.

A seasonally unemployed labourer, Declan O—, makes an (illegal) bet on a light heavyweight boxing match, and wins five pounds. A fortune, to him. The first thing he does is to buy an off-the-peg suit in a sturdy Donegal tweed from Honest Alphonse the Thirty-Shilling Tailor. Also new shoes. Then he goes to the pub, his local, the Princess Beatrice, and downs numberless pints of Guinness. At 11 p.m. the publican, as he must, calls out, 'Last orders!' followed by, 'Time, gentlemen, time!' The labourer staggers out into Hawley

Crescent – what with his mysterious luck and new-found new-spent wealth, not to mention alcohol, he feels immense and fast-slow as his own slant shadow, sublime, formidable, archangelic – and he exercises his privilege of lying down with his head pillowed on the granite kerb and his body on the tarmac.

He is woken, past midnight, by a taxi driver who is trying to park.

'Shift your blooming legs!'

Declan O— stirs his head. He blinks. He examines a pair of queerly unfamiliar black brogues; puzzling greenish trousers . . . 'They're not *my* legs,' as his eyes close and he falls into a light dream.

I*d*

Here is a city which is not a city. It is the countryside. There are farms and fields, and meadows rich with larkspur and eglantine where lovers wander hand in hand, winding brooks, narrow lanes, market gardens invested with parsnip, rhubarb, turnip; not to mention scarecrows, miscellaneous ditches, dung. Also a railway line slashing straight through. Yet this does not detract from the rural quality of the scenery: in some ways it adds to it – the exception that proves the rule. Much the same might be said of the branch lines, the sidings, the cuttings associated with the rail business. Also the major highway, and all the lesser highways. And naturally not everybody in this rural idyll literally works on the land; some are housewives and mothers, teachers, shopkeepers, locomotive repair personnel, machinists in artificial teeth factories, cinema usherettes, operatives of all kinds. Nor is there room for them to live in traditional villas, or hovels, or cottages wreathed in climbing rose. A row of semi-detached houses in the recently fashionable 'Jacobethan' style is considered more than adequate; many reside in maisonettes, back-to-backs, blocks of flats.

Yet the residents of these too consider themselves country types – for no sooner do they trot down the stairs to the ground floor and step out of their front door than they find themselves in the wilds – say, the triangular patch of grass between the car park and John Barnes department store. By no means is all the greenery so limited: Primrose Hill is a decent-sized hummock; Regent's Park is ampler, if more tamed; Hampstead Heath at once vaster and more savage . . . but it should be admitted that many of the millions of inhabitants of this countryside-city have to content themselves, on a daily basis, with a patch of nature the size of a double bed; or one that rests on a windowsill and is no larger than a crib; one that can be lifted in both hands and hugged.

There are even blasphemers who snort that this city cannot be classified as rural at all: notwithstanding the ample scatter of municipal parks, the profusion of florists' establishments, the widespread attention paid to talks about gardening on the wireless . . . but they are wrong. They must be wrong. For it is universally admitted, here, that urban life stunts the proper expression and growth of the individual: one can only truly be oneself when out among nature. The Permanent Under-Secretary at the Ministry of Defence (the Armaments Procurement wizard) cares for nothing, truly, except his prize dahlias.

And, undeniably, the sceptics are in the process of being refuted – as, day by day, the city becomes more rustic. Trenches are being dug along Buckland Crescent in order to create air-raid shelters. Savernake Road is torn up to lay down the foundations of an anti-aircraft artillery emplacement. When The Doktor leans out of his bathroom window and takes a good sniff, he savours the aroma of, among much else, freshly exposed earth – somewhere just out of sight (he is assured) revealed earthworms wriggle.

The Doktor thinks of this city's graveyards (nothing like the Continental orderly places, supervised by a head clerk with a card file): boggy fields sploshed down randomly, where willow and cypress and maybe a straggly blackberry bush burgeon any old how and squirrels are chased by feral cats; where untidiness is considered a proof of sincerity – the bowler-hatted master gardener aims his umbrella at the sub-gardeners (refugee boys from Berlin or Vienna, with little English, who can find no better job and don't get the point of this one) and screams.

And if it goes on like this, in a few years the rural city shall no longer be a dream, a delusion, a collective psychosis, but a fact. The cemetery gardeners shall have gone off to war work, or be interned, peculiarly, as enemy aliens; foxes shall nest in the Constable family tomb; rabbits shall burrow and twitch among Victorians' bones. There shall be more open space than ever: cracked brick shall have returned to clay, concrete to sand; many buildings shall not exist or, if they survive, be a blatant irrelevance. The Doktor's ghost shall stroll through the rough terrain – his attention caught by a damp peeling fragment of floral design wallpaper flapped in the breeze . . . thistle . . . apple sapling . . . rosebay willowherb . . .

The patient, Rosa W—, has been free-associating. Currently she is talking about her husband, Arthur W—, a senior clerk at the head offices of the Midland Bank, in Poultry, who, every afternoon at half past four, enters the Underground (the Northern Line – the black one, on the map) at Bank station, judders along inside it for twenty minutes and exits at either Belsize Park (where there is no park) or Chalk Farm (farm-free, of course) and putters, via the potting shed at 35 England's Lane where he changes into comfortable old clothing, to his garden: he spends the rest of the afternoon and evening happily mulching the sweet peas. Smelling of sweat and soil, he goes to bed late. Early the following morning he washes, dresses, takes the Underground to the office. The patient states she would

rather he were betraying her with some floozy from his secretarial pool; and The Doktor wonders if that might be
arranged: it is a common enough occurrence: on his strolls
through Hampstead Heath he has often encountered semi-
nude couples wrestling behind the bushes. The standard
contraceptive technique is the withdrawal method – much
seed is scattered on the ground. Indeed (thus The Doktor
theorizes) the female partner is only an excuse: the man
shuts his eyes and satisfies his deepest urge: to fornicate
with clods of earth, tree roots, dandelion sap.

While The Doktor has been musing, Rosa W— has
become silent.

While Rosa W— muses, The Doktor remains silent.

The Doktor and the patient wait each other out.

The Doktor and the patient pat silence between them
like a medicine ball.

Silence continues as long as it possibly can.

Then she relates her earliest memory from childhood.

Jetsam

Plaques are affixed to the walls of historic buildings, stating by whom or for whom they were built, in which era. The municipal authorities must have commissioned the installation; at any rate somebody did. Thus we learn that a Kentish Town church is Queen Anne; that a row of shops in Camden is a fine example of Georgian architecture; that the juncture of College Crescent and Finchley Road is the site of an early Victorian coaching inn. No matter that the church is overlaid with Puginesque accretions; that the Camden shops have had their bay windows flattened and their façades vermiculated and rusticated by Edwardian renovators; that the inn site is waste ground (there are plans to dig an Anderson shelter here, that the public may flee underground in the event of an air raid) with not the slightest hint of its Pickwickian heyday – what matters is the moment of creation. Just so, proverbial sayings and folk songs are assigned to some supposed era in which they came into being. Even foodstuffs are dated (a certain recipe for poached peach is associated with a particular performance by an opera singer; a style of cooking chicken is linked to one of Napoleon's battles). Even styles of humour. Even sexual techniques. Even psychopathic syndromes. Even nursery rhymes – children singing *Ring-a-ring-a-roses* are referring, allegedly, to an antique plague.

For it is dogma in this city that whatever happens now is the product of some momentous past event. The military and political developments that keep being announced on the wireless: they must be the upshot of a given historic injustice, say; or a specifiable flaw in a named treaty; or the failure of nerve on the part of so-and-so on such-and-such a date. Esmerelda L—, a fat person, when she permits the Doktor to swing his golden fob watch until she enters a hypnotic trance – it is all for the purpose of discovering that she was battered, at age two months, by a drunken milkman. When a leading homosexual accountant sits in the shade of The Doktor's silence, the invert does so that he may eventually free-associate his way back to having had his favourite teddy bear dissected by prefects at his preparatory school. A minor poet's lyric gift is traceable to his primary school substitute teacher, the charming Miss M—, who on a single Tuesday taught him to write joined-up letters;

having had this explained to him, he is liberated of his urge
to produce incessant verse – pantoum upon rime riche upon
limerick upon ottava rima upon tanka upon sonnet – and
can settle down to a worthwhile career as an advertising
copywriter. Nothing develops gradually, or just is; everything sprang into existence dramatically, traumatically –
everything has a right to have been so inaugurated.

And if no such origin can be found . . . but an origin is
always found!

Take Mr and Mrs P—. Although the circumstances of
their existence are idyllic, they are miserable. They sit side
by side on the couch and weep. How can this be? they ask
The Doktor, who remains in silence, and lets them talk
themselves out. Since they are married, they must initially
have been in love; they would be the first to assume this.
Since they were in love, there must have been a particular
incident that sparked off the romance. For want of better,
Mr P— is willing to recall a time he saved her pet mouse
from a stray cat. She, for her part, remembers an afternoon
he spent in Golders Green without her, and she missed him.
And this is sufficient. True, it would seem they do not love
each other any more or perhaps ever: their mutual feelings
might pass for indifference; but he knows in his heart that
she, beneath her bitterness, adores him; she is sure that he,
despite his boisterousness, is a secret romantic. And so they

think of themselves as an (unhappy) happily married couple. On Saturdays they go for long wordless walks by the canal, in the flickering waterlight, all the way from Little Venice to Camden Lock, along the towpath where donkeys drag housebarges through the gleamy murk while the rat-catcher sings as he lays his traps.

K*iss*

The Doktor is opting for gelato. At the Caffè Venezia on Chalk Farm Road, opposite the railway cutting, he is seated at one of the outside tables, shaded by a table-parasol dyed with the colours of the Italian flag. Nearby, Nic the aged organ-grinder is turning the handle which operates his instrument, causing it to emit an unrecognizable melodious creak; he is accompanied by his chained pet monkey, Shylock, who can jig in tempo. The Doktor dispenses a farthing. The monkey bites the little copper coin; his master snatches it from his paws. As for the confection, be assured it is exquisitely delicious – a *coppa tre* composed of equal parts *fragola*, *zuppa inglese*, and *zabaglione*. It is the hue and texture of muddy slush. It comes in a striped paper cone which is deliciously inedible. It is one of the last gelati of the pre-War era, for in a matter of months Mussolini will invade France, hence the proprietors of the gelateria along with Nic and Nic's ape will be arrested as enemy aliens and dispatched to an internment camp on the Isle of Man, for the duration.

Even as The Doktor sucks and nibbles, and sticks his tongue out to catch a stray drip . . . a few miles to the west, in a suburban laboratory, an impassioned inventor named Geoffrey P— is hard at work. He is mixing wood pulp with seawater ice, and placing the resultant mush in the heart of an industrial freezer. The frozen melange is to be known as, of course, P—ite. The scientist foresees great prospects for this substance. As he is ever ready to point out, it can be manufactured in virtually limitless quantities just about anywhere where trees are in ample supply, as is ice, such as along the coast of Nova Scotia. Floes composed of it may be towed across the north Atlantic, all the way to Britain. These floes will be (he proclaims) unsinkable.

The odd thing is that Geoffrey P— really exists, in the history books at least, and, odder, in three years' time he will manage to infect Winston Churchill, along with not a few of the staff at Combined Operations HQ, with his enthusiasm. Churchill will go so far as to authorize a preliminary study of what shall be referred to as Project Habakkuk: the scheme to moor such a floe in the English Channel, to serve as a kind of aircraft carrier.

And this is not the limit of P—'s vision. Since the enemy

aircraft rely on radar (he will argue), how easy it would be to fool them by constructing a full-size simulacrum of Great Britain, to be tethered permanently in the North Sea.

Think about it, in retrospect. How wonderful it would have been, had it only been tried for real, and had worked. The blitz that shall flatten the docklands of eastern London, should explode only a kind of ice. The churches that shall be destroyed: St Augustine, St Andrew-by-the-Wardrobe, St Vedast . . . only ice should crumble. The flames that shall lick around the rim of St Paul's Cathedral, that shall almost bring down the Monument erected to commemorate the Great Fire of London in 1666, these should rage about nothing but ice. The bombs that shall fall on the House of Commons, and on Buckingham Palace, also the V-1 that shall demolish 12 Maresfield Gardens (only four houses away from The Doktor's) killing a mother and her two infants in the spring of 1943, should destroy ice, and ice, and ice.

However, now, as The Doktor dabs his handkerchief in his beard, mopping up a little fallen *zuppa inglese*, and scribbling annotations in the margin of *The Interpretation of Dreams*, P—ite remains in the early developmental stage. And the Prime Minister is still Neville Chamberlain – though Churchill is dreaming of replacing this namby-pamby government, this country of theirs, with ones constructed in his own image.

And it is hardly likely that The Doktor, in his lifetime, will get to hear of P—ite – since the social circles of the analyst and the inventor are absolutely non-intersecting. Nor does P— consider himself in any wise in need of psychiatric help. Tempting though it is to imagine him prone on the famous couch, having his fantasies extracted and interpreted by the dying Master, it did not and could not ever happen.

Yet, even as The Doktor perches on the rickety folding chair outside Caffè Venezia on this glorious day in late summer, his head in shadow, his knees heated by the sun, he shivers. His head trembles. He slips his thumb inside his mouth, and prods his palate, for the same reason that could-be dreamers notoriously pinch themselves. His lips purse and pucker at passers-by. It is as if, conceivably, by some terrible mistake he has been sent to the wrong London – the Victoria station where his train arrived was the one made of ice, the ice-porter assisted with his ice-luggage and hailed the ice-taxi which took him to his ice-suburb, where he settled in the ice-house; ice-patients deliver themselves of ice-thoughts on the ice-couch . . . he is stranded forever on this slowly melting giant dirty berg.

Jones parks his Bentley Voyager behind the Bull and Bush. He carries out his black bag, just in case. He walks around to the passenger side, and assists The Doktor in descending to ground level. The Doktor is in reasonable health considering, smart in a pepper-and-salt overcoat, and once his arm has been taken by Jones, walks without too much difficulty over the wasteland and meadow towards Hampstead Heath. Sunshine sparkles off twists of discarded cigarette foil and chicken bones.

They can already hear the noises – really just an undifferentiated clamour, all its rumbling and shrieking components whisked into one – but once they have clambered over the grassy hillock they see it stretched out in front of them. It is the funfair – the one that always takes place on this day every year, prospect of war or no war. A small Ferris wheel winds into the sky. Steam-organ music groans and bangs. A roundabout drills into the earth.

'To your taste?' says Jones.

He is not sure this really was such a good idea. His first thought had been to go to the theatre (they say the new farce at the Aldwych, *Spotted Dick*, has them rolling in the aisles) or the cinema (The Doktor might have taken a shine to *Snow White*), but then again . . .

'Yes,' says The Doktor.

In truth, he is an old hand at funfairs – he took his children when small to the one in Vienna, on the Prater; and this example is nothing special. In fact, at first glance it seems a poor specimen, disorganized. But then, there is something peculiarly pleasing about its very pettiness, its muddle.

They have been descending into the heart of the fair. They are in the food sector. A variety of booths press close around. The odours are potent. A substantial notice states *FRYING TONIGHT*. With vim customers shake malt vinegar over fish and chips; the greasy triangles of newspaper in which these are contained are dropped afterwards on the earth – crumpled, partially see-through, illegible.

A stall presents mussels, clams, cockles, jellied eels. The Doktor peers at these last with glee.

'I dissected that.'

'I really don't think . . .'

'My very first research paper was on its grooved lobulate testicular organ.'

'. . . they're altogether appropriate. Little sharp bits inside. You're better off with winkles.'

Other booths offer meat pies . . . ice cream . . . mashed potato . . . apples coated with toffee . . . ginger beer . . .

The Doktor is squinting at a man dipping a wooden splint into a fast-spinning vat of pink-dyed spun sugar. The fluffy substance accumulates on the stick, like yarn on a spindle. The Doktor hands over a penny and buys a portion. He holds up the stick, examining his purchase from various angles.

'We call it –' says Jones.

'The name is neither here nor there.'

The Doktor opens his mouth wide and plunges the tip in. Pink filaments mesh with his beard.

The Doktor has a giant head.

Jones's is tiny and squat.

The Doktor is needle-thin and lanky.

Jones's shoulders are broad as a bison's.

The Doktor's beard extends way down, merging with his groin.

Jones's upper half is nipped off from his lower.

The Doktor's spectacles reflect the reflections.

And some boys and girls are also in the Hall of Mirrors –

skipping about, peering and grimacing in every glass, ignoring the two older men – interested only in their own transformations, laughing or pretending to laugh.

Consider an entertainment in which people climb into electric cars and ram hard into one another. Sometimes a number of cars collide, become jammed, trapped: nobody can escape. Wild music plays. The Doktor stands on the brink, looking on.

Jones (who had been captain of his school First Eleven) paces well back so as to have a decent run-up, then hurls the cricket ball in the orthodox overarm action. It hits the coconut hard – which however only wobbles slightly on its perch.

Now The Doktor spends a halfpenny on a ball. He rolls it about his palm. His middle finger wraps around the stitched crease. His left hand gropes and clutches Jones's lapel – for the sake of maintaining his balance. The ball smashes into the coconut and knocks it to the ground. Cracked, its vegetable milk seeps away.

'In the Great War I was taught the elements of grenade throwing – all part of basic training,' The Doktor murmurs, as he receives his coconut. He hands it to Jones, for safekeeping.

'Did you ever kill anybody?'

'I was commissioned as a physician, of course.'

*

At the shooting gallery, The Doktor pierces the target bang on the moustache. He wins a teddy bear. This also is carried out by Jones.

The ping-pong ball plops into the glass bowl. Thus The Doktor is awarded a live goldfish.

The Doktor saunters through the crowds of children and grown-ups, the occasional soldier or sailor or airman on leave, the odd tramp, pickpocket, spy, dog; he is relishing the gaudiness and the seediness, the flare and shade, the electric energy, the thrill. Meanwhile Jones – a native bearer, of sorts – struggles under the bulky composite burden of the nut, fish, stuffed doll, steam train (this last, a Hornby scale model, was The Doktor's reward at the darts booth), not to speak of his own black bag.

'Enough,' Jones says. 'Let's leave some prizes for others.'

But The Doktor sees no reason to do so. A certain imaginative ruthlessness has taken him far.

Jones suggests, 'Perhaps we should . . . er, instead . . .'

The Doktor says nothing. He is waiting for Jones to reveal himself.

Jones pays his threepence and sits down on the squirrel. The Doktor is on the neighbouring swan. Let the steam-organ music commence: 'Sailor's Hornpipe' segueing into 'Golliwogg's

Cakewalk' into Beethoven's Fifth. The merry-go-round acceler-
ates gradually – the animals drift simultaneously round-and-
round and up-and-down. Jones relaxes. His baggage is fairly
secure on his lap, and whatever may happen in the course of the
ride is hardly his responsibility. The Doktor also is enjoying the
journey – the recurrence – the jerky overview of this suburb of
the fair, this temporary encampment, this collective dream, precious by virtue of being tawdry, tawdry by virtue of being
thought precious. Elsewhere, a rude girl on a cow sticks her
tongue out at an infant boy. He, his mouth crammed with a
toffee apple, clings hard to the crest of his turkey and stares at
the revolving bobbing world in mute wonder and terror.

And when the music has faded out and the merry-go-round
ticks to a standstill, The Doktor is slumped against the swan's
lengthy sculptured neck, his face distorted, panting. A panicky
operative scampers about the wooden animals: 'Is there a doctor
in the merry-go-round?' But Jones recognizes the familiar symptoms. It is with a certain relief that he takes command. He
crouches beside the swan so that The Doktor may piggyback on
his shoulders and be led away.

As for the prizes, somebody must have stolen them but aban-
doned them – for they were dumped in the Hall of Mirrors.
There they remain, static, arrayed under the flat electric light,
unclaimed for the duration – separate objects, worthy of

inconclusive thought, multi-distorted – animal/vegetable/mineral – totems; fetishes; extracts from an encyclopedia of dream symbols – without meaning or with too many meanings.

A carthorse browses in a blackberry bush. It is free from its traces. It rubs its neck against the side of a gaily striped caravan: a poster is glued to the front:

I KNOW WHAT I KNOW
ADVISER TO THE CROWNED HEADS OF EUROPE
LOVE! HAPPINESS! SICKNESS!

The fair carries on. Fun-lovers mill not far from the caravan . . .

Inside, Jones is unlocking his black bag. The Doktor is floundering across a faded orange chintz armchair; his jaw is twitching; the agony in his palate is a succession of sharp stabs. The fortune-teller, sitting on her bed by the back wall, is coaxing, 'I'll do you yours for a sovereign . . .' Jones is drawing 3 cc of morphine (5 per cent dilution) into a syringe ('. . . or why not round it up to a guinea?') and injecting it directly into the vein behind The Doktor's left ear. 'It'll cost you a sovereign anyroad,' the fortune-teller is whining. A jangle of silver half-crowns is being thrust into her hand. The pain is fast subsiding . . .

. . . Subsiding . . .

The Doktor breathes slower. He is enthroned in the armchair, dopy, staring at nothing.

Jones squeezes The Doktor's shoulder. 'I'll just and go and get the Bentley,' as he leaves.

The fortune-teller is alone with The Doktor.

She stashes her takings in a tea caddy under the bed.

She steps forward and presses her hand on the old man's forehead.

She tightens her lips.

She pulls a bright gown around his shoulders; it bulks and bunches on top of his overcoat. She drapes a dim shawl over his head and around his neck. She stuffs his pink-tainted beard inside his collar, cravat-wise.

She draws the curtains.

She stares into his eyes.

Then, satisfied she has done all that can reasonably be expected of her, in the light of her own code of honour and sense of duty to self, and that she has been adequately paid for her time, she lies on her bed, climbs under the blanket, and falls asleep.

The Doktor is in the armchair, drifting in and out of consciousness.

The door opens and a girl of perhaps fourteen enters. She squints into the gloom.

'I'll give you sixpence.'

The Doktor does not answer.

'You tell me my fate, and I'll cross your palm with silver.'

No reply.

'All right, then. I'll cough up a whole bob.'

The Doktor is silent.

She is reluctant to bid more, reluctant to leave . . . for a while she teeters between the two impulses. Then:

'But you've got to be real, mind you. I'm not paying for no lies. Love. Happiness. Sickness. You give me that and I'll . . . Yeah, how much do you know? . . . Really?'

Lion

A cloud occupies the neighbourhood. 'Fog' would be the normal word for it – but that would give the wrong impression. Fog implies an unclarity, yes, but at least a reasonably uniform one: all perspectives are blurred alike: a common limitation: a sense of fair play. Whereas this damp opaqueness, it has drifted down to pavement level and has stuck in place; its overall shape is something like a giant plaited loaf; it is distinctly localized. Elsewhere the day is a fine one – Compayne Gardens and East Heath Road, Jack Straw's Castle and the boating lake, no scrap of mist is reported there. Even within the district, those on the tops of the tallest buildings – the steeplejack repairing the lead weather-proofing on St John's; the old woman who lives at the summit of Downshire Hill – are above it all: they blink in the sunshine and look down on a layer of cushioned white-ness. But here, below, pedestrians hold their arms out like sleepwalkers, cyclists walk their machines, drivers sound their horns.

This cannot last. By noon the sun has burned the cloud away, from the top down. First visible are spires, towers: the crosses and weathercocks and lightning conductors that perch on them; then gables, slate roofing material (roofs bob and toss like ships on an off-white sea); the signs above shops, and then the shops themselves . . . A curious disjunction here. For what is inside the building does not in general correspond to what is carved on its pediment. For all that the outside may state *Sweet Shop*, what is on offer may be cleaning materials. A sign for *Midland Bank* may be belied by caged dachshund puppies prancing on minced newspaper; goldfish; parrots. *Rose & Crown* may conceal a church. *Jackson, Butchers* may lead one to expect sawdust clotted with occasional trickles – yet the establishment below might be a milliner's where fashionable housewives admire themselves in a triple cheval glass as they adjust a feathered paisley turban, 'Do you think this is quite *me*?' What sounds like a rumbling stomach at an Elsworthy Road dinner party might actually be the roar of a lion in the Regent's Park zoo.

For this is a city where the outside cannot be assumed to correspond to the inside; in fact seldom does. As a rule they are unrelated. The tyrant of the secretarial pool Miss S— may very well be; yet at home how meekly she warms her aged mother, Mrs S—,'s slippers in front of the gas fire, and scrapes the slightest burnt patches off the old lady's toasted crumpets. A torrid Latin lover, Juan O—, wipes the sweat from his swarthy brow and puts on his wing-tips, pinstripes, and bowler: he goes to work as a teller in a bank, and spends the day counting money; when he has finished stacking the five-pound banknotes, he inverts them: their obverse is blank – they could pass for sheets of writing paper. Mary H—, the fruiterer's assistant by day, by night is a devotee of chiliastic left-wing politics.

To those who come from more unified cities, this division between interior and exterior may seem bizarre – as if a banana, on being peeled, were to reveal a mackerel; an old Bible, opened, to contain only a bad smell – yet it is normal here, and not a matter of happenstance: it is considered proper. To link the two halves of one person's life would be regarded as taboo, almost incestuously so. When the rat-catcher is in the chess club, neither he nor his fellow players would dream of discussing arsenical bait; no more than, down in the sewer, would he mention his subtle theoretical analysis of a knight–bishop versus rook endgame. Let no talk of cavities distract the dancing dentist.

Nevertheless, even here, the outside and the inside do sometimes merge – if only in memory. Liquorice and silver polish. Chequebooks and ant eggs. Beer and prayer. Hatpins and pressed tongue. Wisps of fog trail at ankle level across the paving stones: shoppers trudge on clouds. The teller weeps in his cage; during her lunch hour the secretarial supervisor types *Help!* on a sheet of used blotting paper; the fruiterer's assistant breaks into bursts of spontaneous martial song . . . Begging the question: What could be that sad about banknotes? In which way is a typewriter ribbon to be feared? How come apples are so delightful?

Marco Polo

The Doktor coughs. It is dusk. The blackout curtains are drawn. Summer is grinding itself down. The wireless has been crackling about what has been declared between one side and another side, good versus bad, this versus that – perhaps it counts as what they call a phoney war: nobody actually fights; he is feeling none too well himself. He pulls his crocheted muffler in the MacDowell tartan (gift from a grateful patient) closer around his neck and shoulders. He broods over a back issue of the *Jahrbuch für Psychoanalytische und Psychopathologische Forschungen*, frowning at an article with suspiciously Adlerian tendencies. He slides his thumb down the index, taking refuge in the reliable logic of alphabetical order. He quavers on the rattan rocking chair.

He rises – by leaning so far forward as to, as it were, tip himself out. He staggers upright. And over to the fire, where the coal has already been laid in the grate.

He rips off page viii of the footnotes, and bends it into a spill. Against the granite surround of the fireplace he scrapes the tip of a vesta. Which flares up and emits a sulphurous stink – but the *Jahrbuch* fails to catch light. (It cannot be denied that psychoanalytical journals tend to be somewhat moist.) He rips off a strip of *The Times*. He lights another match, and uses the newsprint (an editorial advocating proceeding with firm caution and cautious firmness) instead. Adequately flammable. The spill is flaming: he drops it: he chivvies the fiery scrap with the poker. The coals soon catch fire.

He is practically choking! The smoke, instead of rising up the chimney, is curving back into the consulting room. The flue must be blocked – a bird's nest up there; an excessive quantity of soot; there is never a sweep around when you need one.

He hurls the contents of a chamber pot onto the grate.

He totters back, and bangs open the door.

And further back into the corridor. And through the front door to the Welcome mat, the porch, the crazy-paved garden path . . .

. . . into the city. He suffers the brief illusion that, with his little malformed fire, he has smoked out the entire city – for it, too, is rendered semi-opaque. It is foggy! Yes, this city is notorious for its fogs – even those people who have never been here, who have never wanted to be here, who never will come here if they can help it, know all about its brumousness, its fantastic murk – yet in all The Doktor's time here there has scarcely been even a decent mist, until now at last.

Yet, on second glance, the place is not as nebulous as all that. He can see clear, by starlight, to the box hedges fronting the houses on the far side of the road. This so-called fog is no thicker than a mountain vapour, no more opaque than a net curtain. No matter: surely a city can be famously foggy without actually having a great deal of fog – just as Casanova was not, in fact, an unusually ardent lover.

A scream.

The thud of fast footsteps.

A police whistle.

Down the street, the squarish black shape of a taxicab slowly looming past.

Silhouettes projected on the bay window of the front parlour at number 8 of the two rotund lodgers picking a fight.

That genial housekeeper from number 17, Mrs Q—, in her tweed overcoat and carpet slippers, stomping about with a carving knife clutched in her right hand.

And these activities are quite in order (The Doktor realizes) for, during the fog, the normal constraints of civilized urban life do not apply. The fog of London serves the same function as the 'domino' costumes once worn by Venetians during their carnival: since everybody was anonymous, anybody could carry out a secret desire without fear of detection. Just so, in this fog city, the most respectable of gentlemen of leisure might stroll out to Whitechapel, say, have relations with a prostitute, rip open her womb, dispose of his bloody knife in the Thames, take a Turkish bath, go home – and wake up the following morning: the day and his conscience equally clear. Similarly a cocaine-addicted violinist might prowl the streets, his deerstalker cap firm on his skull, his magnifying glass raised at a jaunty angle, in the capacity of a brilliant private detective – but, once the fog has lifted, return to his wastrel life once more. An amateur chemist is entitled to swallow his own potion – commit a gamut of vices – and be right as rain after the fog has drifted away, suffering no more lasting effect than a faint hangover.

Interestingly, the Venetian domino covered only part of the body, and would scarcely have served to disguise the posture let alone the voice – however it was a strict convention that no one should admit to recognizing a masked reveller, and whatever was done then was held to take place in a separate world, with imprecise identities, without guilt or remorse or obligation.

In fact, it seems that the more unconvincing the disguise

the more conviction is to be placed in it: the thinner the fog
the stronger the belief in its cloaking power: the more the
reality of this city is denied, the more easily it can enter into
its delusory state. (An analogy is to be drawn with schizoid
imaginings – The Doktor muses; it tends to be whores who
claim they are Greta Garbo; weaklings that they are Charles
Atlas; virgins are Mary Magdalene; Jews are Jesus Christ.)

The Doktor seizes the opportunity to investigate the fog
city. He trudges over to Finchley Road, and waves down a
number 13 bus. The great scarlet double-decker shudders to
a halt. He clambers – helped by the conductor – up onto
the platform. The conductor presses a red bull's-eye, causing an electric bell to ring – and alerting the driver to
debrake. The bus lurches off slowly towards the centre of
the city.

Meanwhile The Doktor is climbing the spiral stairs to the
upper level. The stairs keep rocking; the way is steep and
narrow and dim, as if ascending to a belfry.

But at last he is up here. He slumps down in a corner seat
at the back.

He eyes the other passengers, a dozen or so individuals,
each politely ignoring fellow travellers.

The conductor, a middle-aged woman with blonded hair
under a headscarf, smoking a Woodbine, at last approaches.
Mumbling: 'Where are you going, dearie?'

He holds up an index finger.

'One penny, love?'

He nods.

Her machine, dangling at mid bosom, tinkles and wags. It absorbs his plump brown coin. It extrudes a fragment of cheap paper, faintly printed with letters and numbers. She vanishes.

The Doktor clutches his prize, his possession, his fortune . . . as the bus quivers and wobbles through sombre urban streets.

After a while he notices that the bus – far from following its appointed route south towards Baker Street – has deviated along Adelaide Road, and is heading east and then north again! True, some of the street signs have been removed (precaution against spies and enemy parachutists) but if even he, an alien, knows where he is, how can the driver be so mistaken?

But soon all becomes clear to The Doktor. For the bus grinds to a halt in front of a semi-detached mock-Tudor residence on Lambolle Place. A minute later the driver comes up the stairs, his arms out as if making his way through pitch blackness, and announces, 'Can't see a bloody thing in this fog. Going to have to wait it out.'

The conductor soon follows him upstairs. Her ticket machine is rocking from side to side; her hands are in front of her, groping . . . descending like spiders on the driver's haunch.

This seems to be the signal. The various passengers stumble and wibble-wabble through the dense fog of their imagination, up to other passengers. Items of clothing are peeled back or removed. Bodies are juxtaposed in various arrangements. The padded sprung seats creak and shake. Faint gasps disturb the night. Whatever may be happening on board, it is unseeable, unknowable to any native of that fog city. In the entire double-decker only The Doktor remains seated in his place, upright, watching, taking mental notes, his itchy muffler knotted tight around his neck.

No-*Man*

Posit a city where psychology fails. Or rather, it is irrelevant here. For the inhabitants, though they exhibit the full range of symptoms, do not possess any syndrome which may be analysed by the techniques of psychoanalysis. Not just that The Doktor's theories and methods are inapplicable – though they certainly are – but also those of all his rivals and colleagues and of the band of his faithful disciples (the 'beards' – as they were nicknamed in Vienna) and of his rebellious ex-disciples (the 'clean shavers'). If The Doktor cannot interpret or treat this city – no more could adherents of the schools of Jung or of Adler, of Janet or Wagner-Jauregg . . . The Doktor possesses an *Unbedenklichkeitserklärung* (literally: a 'doubtless-ness declaration') which he was obliged to purchase for 31,329 Reichsmarks before being allowed to emigrate. It is an official statement that nothing could be proved against him. About the best that could be said in his favour.

And yet – this is the paradox – it is not as if the subjects were emotionally inadequate, or lacking in interior complexity, or more than usually freakish. It seems however that no causation is involved, no link between stimulus and consequence, origin and outcome. As if the unconscious exists but cannot be sketched or diagrammatized – only illustrated, conceivably, by a pointilliste: a dab of this colour here – empty space – a different colour there – emptiness – and now another different colour . . .

Prospective patients ring The Doktor's door bell. And he has to turn them away. He has to swear at them, '*Unbedenklichkeitserklärung Schmunbedenklichkeitserklärung!*' For all they have to offer is a jumble of unanalysables.

Ask whether this city could exist (The Doktor's nightmare), could it?

Ask whether a city could have locations but be unmappable?

Ask the way of an old man at the corner of Maresfield Gardens and Nutley Terrace, 'Can you tell me how I should get to . . .?' – and his head will shake, judder, from the crown of his hat to the base of his beard, unable, though he knows the streets by heart, to give directions, unable to express directions, in a city made up of (not necessarily in this or any given order) Finchley Road – melancholia – Fitzjohn's Avenue – pointless laughter – College Crescent – rage – Akenside

Road – nail-biting – Frognal Lane – sleepiness – Lower Merton Rise – anger – Sumpter Close – unjustified hope – Elsworthy Road – fear – Lyndhurst Terrace – insomnia – Prince Albert Road – hatred – Adelaide Road – obsessive washing of the hands – Downshire Hill – bed-wetting – Goldhurst Terrace – glossolalia – Maresfield Gardens – delusions of grandeur.

Orchestra

A nexus of residential streets in a northern suburb of the city. It is still quite early. Diluted sunlight is seeping in. It happens to be Thursday. Throughout this district, outside every house, in front of the side entrance or by the trap door which leads only to the coal cellar, positioned on the grey paving material, reposes a lone hollow cylinder or, more usually, several. Formed of corrugated, unstainless steel, the cylinders are as tall as, and wider than, a seven-year-old-boy; their lids, also of steel, would serve such a boy as a shield for purposes of war play. They are arranged in casual groupings – acquaintances who have struck up a gossipy conversation. They are painted with street numbers, to pre-empt possible confusion. They contain, of course, just rubbish.

For the residents of this neighbourhood are required, at this hour every week, to put out their dustbins – else they would not be emptied until another seven days have passed. It is best for this chore to have been done earlier, before breakfast, so as to have been dealt with already. But some laggards have left it until the last moment. The financial director of a struggling yet promising import/export concern is hastening to expel his bin – before he rushes off to work. He is a considerable person and wishes the world to know it: his suit is seriously black; his pince-nez roosts between his eyes like a permanent frown. As he heaves his heavy-laden bin, he ponders the rise and fall of interest rates. A maid of all work, dressed in the traditional black-and-white uniform, has deliberately left a button or two undone on her blouse. She manoeuvres her virtually empty bin along the passageway and into the street. She glances up and down; she is hoping that nice policeman with the pink face will come by on his beat. She hauls the dustbin in a sensual dance, a tango . . . She switches to a faster rhythm: a quickstep . . . a Lindy hop . . .

Unconsciously she is moving in tempo with a faint steady noise, something like a drumbeat, echoing through the district. It is a company of seasoned soldiers, professionals in the Royal Engineers, marching down from Primrose Hill. A sergeant is calling, 'Lef-ri! Lef-ri! Lef-ri!' The consonants he swallows must be accumulating in his chest. The company is marching in step as, by regulation, it must. Only its sound exists here: for the army in the flesh is quite distant, and shows no sign of coming closer.

But now its noise is overlaid by an elaborate cacophony. The dustmen's vehicle, maladjusted on a strained suspension, comes roaring slowly down the road. The driver and his mate are at the front; two assistants are at the back, perched on the mudguards, unsteadily. The vehicle brakes. The assistants jump off.

It is they – a Scotsman and a native cockney – who actually collect the bins. They carry them, peculiarly, behind their backs, in a way designed to minimize lumbar strain. Next, working as a pair they lift the lids, and tip the contents into the maw of the machine. They return the empty bins to where they came from, roughly. As they work, they all but ignore the surroundings – the façades of the respectable houses, the plane trees and the flowering cherries, the curious maid and incurious businessman – for they know appearances are irrelevant, delusory. What is real is rubbish. Under its weight, they grunt.

When, suddenly, the Scot drops a bin almost on the toe of his colleague – who just manages to grab it – and in that instant the cockney has a mystic vision: he is Jacob wrestling with the Angel. Meanwhile the financial director gazes lustfully at the maid. Who is, momentarily, a little girl playing hopscotch: she jumps to a nearby paving stone.

And then, a split second later, the day continues. Assorted garbage tumbles out of the upturned bin. The director climbs into his Daimler. The maid strokes her own cleavage and scans the horizon for her policeman.

And perhaps, a few minutes in the future, there will once more be a brief flash of deviant activity – and normality will resume once more. This is only to be expected. For, in this city, people do not possess a consistent personality. Yes, as a general rule, it is possible to categorize them – but there are always discontinuities, unexpected (even to themselves) thoughts and actions. Sometimes, briefly, anybody is liable to behave like anybody else.

And this may or may not cause problems. Consider the pair of lovers strolling on the grassy slope of Primrose Hill. He is training for the law, articled in a barrister's chambers. He is a most determined and ambitious young fellow. His beloved is a haberdasher's assistant. She is not, by common consent, beautiful; and she is, in terms of the class system, undeniably 'below' him; but what links them is that she too is extremely ambitious, for him. So, on this day of liberty (he is allowed Thursday off, to pursue his studies) as they enjoy the sun and the mild breeze, they consider various stratagems whereby he might ingratiate himself with a certain influential King's Counsel at his Inn of Court.

'Possibly . . .' she suggests.

'In the event that . . .' he agrees.

'If . . .' she asserts.

In the course of their walk they have approached the Edith Cavell Memorial Patisserie, run by a team of widows who fled Brussels during the Great War. The lovers stare at the extended awning, the window with baked products temptingly arrayed behind it. They make interrogative sounds, in order to decide if they should stop by here. They examine each other's translucent reflection in the pane.

Suddenly the man, out of the blue, blurts, 'Belgians!'

'Yes, my dear?'

'Bloody Belgians, they eat horses!'

He points at a glistening chocolate eclair, prominently visible through the vitrine. He compares it to part of a horse's anatomy.

The woman is puzzled. She is dizzy with incomprehension. Why on earth is her respectable lover making such crude banter? She is at a loss – as if he were leading her over a cliff. But her puzzlement lasts just an instant. She jumps over the cliff with him. She too becomes silly: she neighs.

And he neighs.

And she caps his joke with a yet sillier remark on an equine theme.

And he caps hers.

And then she is serious again, stern. 'Regarding the case of Rex versus Jimpson . . .'

Now it is his turn to be baffled – but rapidly he catches on, and he responds to her legal question.

For their occasional interludes of mutual zaniness serve only to bind them closer. Were their moods perfectly aligned, their relationship would be mechanically perfect and hence boring and transient. Were their moods utterly misaligned they would be incompatible. But provided a moderate degree of misalignment is maintained, a necessary irrationality, they will remain a contented couple. There is every prospect that (providing they both survive the War) he will qualify as a barrister, and in due course be promoted to King's Counsel, and in the fullness of time become a judge – and she shall be a judge's wife.

Meanwhile the rhythmic beat has ceased. The sergeant has yelled, 'At ease!' The Other Ranks are no longer march-ing in step. Soon they will be back in strict tempo, but for a while they are not. The reason is simply this: they are advancing by way of the Chalk Farm railway bridge – and it is a strict regulation that soldiers must break step when crossing such a structure – lest it be set into resonant vibration, and break.

P*ig*

A news vendor has surrounded himself with man-high stacks of newspapers, as if to barricade himself in, or establish a makeshift air-raid shelter. There is a cranny between the *Herald*s and the *Daily Worker*s, just sufficient for him to accept payment and give change. This man is here every morning, where Finchley Road cuts into College Crescent. He sells his *Financial Times*-es and his *Sketche*s, his *Daily Telegraph*s and his *Punch*es and his *Illustrated London News*-es; by the afternoon he is moderately exposed. He wears his cap tugged down over his ears, its side-flaps lowered to minimize his field of view; he does little except grunt and receive his coppers. The Doktor has never granted him any particular attention, or indeed bought any of his papers.

But this morning he almost does.

The Doktor waits his turn, behind the other customers.

Each buys a newspaper of some sort, glances at it, and walks away. Many fold their paper, the better to view a section dealing with some issue other than politics. A particular type of man examines the sports as a priority; certain women the fashion. An old person hastens to scan the obituary pages; a middle-aged the Marriage announcements; a young the Births – to see if anybody he knows has been born lately? What strikes The Doktor is the imperturbability of the citizens: how come – given that what they hold in their hands is the news itself, the latest news – they do not gasp or faint or cry out?

The solution must be: this city is inhabited by absolute egoists . . .

. . . just like every other city. (Once, on a lecture tour in America, The Doktor had explained that the dream expresses the wishes of the Ego alone. After the lecture he had been confronted by a delegation from a Women's Club: 'People may be selfish in Europe, but I assure you, Professor, we Americans are altruistic, even in our sleep!') A shop girl buys an *Express*, glances at the headlines, and smiles – because a floorwalker has recently told her she has nice hair. A man in the insurance business has a sore spot on the roof of his mouth; he tucks his *Telegraph* in his attaché case: he will leave it until later. A graphic designer folds her *Sketch* into a triangle. An influenza-struck banker sneezes over the Wanteds. A chemist frowns at a From Our Own Correspondent: a toenail of his is ingrowing. An under-housemaid tears up yesterday's news into rectangles, to serve as toilet paper; she concentrates on her task.

Yet these good people are not solipsists. They display the healthy Ego which every sane adult should possess. They cannot be blamed. A schoolboy is seriously immersed in a comic book; as he reads each page, he tugs and peels it off, the way you eat an artichoke. The Doktor reaches the front of the queue.

On second thoughts he does not buy a paper; he would rather not read it, today. At the last moment he veers aside. He dawdles awhile beside the mounds of assembled newsprint. Commuters and shoppers rush past him, on their way to the nearby florist's, the greengrocer, the bus stop, the Underground.

He is feeling a little chill . . . the sun duly comes out from behind a chimneypot, and blazes directly on The Doktor.

But soon he is overheated . . . whereupon a puff of nimbo-cirrus obscures the sun.

But now he is cool again . . . again the sun beats down, as it should.

And too warm . . . Saved by another entitlement of cloud.

And too cold . . . And too cold . . .

Drizzle drops on The Doktor.

And drizzle keeps falling. He wipes his spectacles on his coat sleeve, uselessly.

And falling . . .

The Doktor unfurls his black umbrella, erects and expands it, and, holding it close over his head, blots out most of this terrible world.

Less than an hour ago, at dusk, while attempting to brush his beard, The Doktor experienced severe twinges followed by a violent pincer-pain inside his head (in the vicinity of the keratotic region of the palato-glossal fold – in The Doktor's professional judgment) – naturally Jones came as soon as he could, and administered a subcutaneous injection of 2.3 cc of 5 per cent morphine.

The dose would have been sufficient to make a lesser man sleep; but The Doktor sits on the end of the couch, in a dreamy state, panting slowly.

'Help me.'

Jones is bending his head low, listening.

'Of course. Whatever is required. Has the sensation abated?'

The Doktor gestures.

Jones finds the bedpan in the bookcase, tucked behind volumes XII–XIII of Jellife & White: *Diseases of the Nervous System*.

Jones reflects: when he had first decided to become a disciple of this great thinker; when he had gone out to Vienna to study under him; and later to rescue him: to assist him in fleeing to this country, this city, this room, this world; he had never expected he would one day serve as The Doktor's valet – nurse – parent.

He deals with The Doktor's urgent physical need.

'If you like, I could feed you . . . perhaps a few spoonfuls of porridge?'

The Doktor does not assent. What with the difficulty of keeping the prosthesis clean, eating is more trouble than it is worth.

Jones is concerned. The man must eat . . . yet it would not do to press food upon him against his desire. It is bad enough having to take on the roles of the other family members – the last thing Jones wants is to turn into a Jewish mother.

The Doktor's head sways.

Jones grasps him by the shoulders.

Just a few weeks ago, Jones was still managing to take The Doktor on short trips outside his home: this would hardly be possible now; his condition is deteriorating fast. Jones tightens his grip, helping the man stay upright.

The Doktor is murmuring something – about love, money, history; and Jones understands at once. For The Doktor's reminiscences are at least as familiar to him as his own. The Doktor is recalling his summons, a decade ago, from Sam Goldwyn who offered a hundred thousand dollars if only The Doktor would advise on a motion picture about Great Lovers Through The Ages, from Antony and Cleopatra on.

Jones interjects, 'He is famous for saying "Include me out" and "In two words: im-possible".'

'No . . . I said that.'

'You would have been rich.'

'A star.'

The Doktor enunciates the potent tri-syllable: 'Hollywood.'

Jones chooses his words with care. 'Well, yes. I suppose you might have appeared in a . . . er . . . cameo role. Acting a psychiatrist, probably.'

'I would have played myself,' says The Doktor.

'You would have played yourself,' says Jones.

The discussion is becoming delicate. Jones glances around the room, in search of some other topic of conversation. A Mycenaean stirrup jar. An illustrated edition of the Brothers Grimm's *Hans in Glück* leaning against *Jude the Obscure*. The tall French window in which the interior is reflected: projecting, as it were, another consulting room out over the garden – a duplicate secretaire loaded with Greek and Egyptian idols; an understudy of the couch draped with an oriental rug; doppelgängers of Jones and The Doktor themselves – all intercut with and body-doubled by the grass, the dahlia bed, the cherry tree.

Jones is saved from having to comment further by a timely interruption. It is the mantel clock, its dial painted with an Alp –

souvenir from a mountaineering holiday. A wooden bird emerges and retreats through a flapping door, while an interior mechanism produces the requisite two-tone call – repeated nine times.

The Doktor makes his wishes known.

Jones raises his eyebrows.

The Doktor succeeds in making a deprecatory cluck.

Jones does his duty. He takes three dog biscuits out of the tin on the secretaire, and goes in search of his master's chow. Which, however, is reluctant to be approached; it cowers under the desk, and the love seat, and behind the French window's blackout curtains, and scampers about The Doktor's ankles, barking softly. Jones goes down on his stomach, woofs to attract attention, and pushes the food over the dusty floorboards, under the sagging couch-frame, towards the beast's blue tongue and sharp teeth. Next he fills the little yellow watering can, and takes care of the pot of narcissus, the hyacinths, soldier orchid, rubber tree.

The Doktor has been staring down between his knees at the pattern in the carpet, to steady himself.

Jones clears his throat. 'Shall I read out your correspondence?'

The Doktor makes no answer.

'Would you like to sleep?'

A whisper: 'Clean me.'

Jones stirs the fire with a poker. Then he goes to fetch hot water. Down a corridor (following the Doktor's directions) and through a door. The kitchen. An admirable, orderly, if curiously antiseptic, place. He puts a kettle on the gas range, and waits for it to boil. All these items here, too many to absorb at once, distinct yet multiple – colander and rolling pin and potato-masher and cheese-grater and *bain-marie* and pastry brush and ladle and . . . And this is just in the one room! How many rooms there must be in this house, as many as in Bluebeard's, recessed, hitherto scarcely guessed at.

A dozen small jars, each containing a brownish or reddish or pale dust of sorts, unlabelled, are lined up on a wooden rack. Jones lifts the lids, and sniffs. The various spices are thereby identified. But the question remains: why are they set out thus and in no other fashion? Surely each detail of The Doktor's kitchen arrangements must have significance? Jones cracks the code. He murmurs the names in his master's original language. *'Gewürznelke. Kardamom. Muskatblüte. Muskatnuss. Zimt.'* Aha, alphabetical order! As arbitrary as they come, nevertheless not without its uses. What would a telephone directory or an encyclopedia or an index to a Collected Works be without it? Even a dream-book has need of it, to cast a skein of logic over the unconscious. It divides up; it sets out; it offers us marvellous juxtapositions. That there is no ultimate pattern yet what we have suffices, is the moral it teaches us.

Jones re-alphabetizes The Doktor's spice rack. He hums

Britishly. He shuffles and shifts the containers, translating as he goes. There is less to it than one might think. The final spice swings round to the beginning; what had been first now fits in the middle. He pats the containers into precise alignment, like a chess player performing his *j'adoube*. *Quod erat demonstrandum. Honi soit qui mal y pense.*

Cardamom – Cinnamon – Clove – Mace – Nutmeg.

The kettle whistles. He pours the steaming water into a galvanized iron tub, dilutes the contents with an equal quantity of tap water, and pushes it steadily back up the corridor.

The tub is on the consulting room hearth – and The Doktor is within it, crouched, having his back scrubbed.

'I've just remembered another Goldwynism,' Jones says. '"Begin with an earthquake and rise to a climax."'

The Doktor nods his approval.

'Which reminds me of the news on the wireless about . . .'

But The Doktor is no mood to hear. His large head shifts restlessly.

Finally: 'I have always been alone . . .'

'Well, hardly.'

'. . . with you . . .'

'Actually you're sharing this house with your –'

'Alone,' The Doktor insists.

In silence Jones rubs the soapy flannel up and down the

arms, the armpits, across the wrinkled scrawny chest with its sparse white hairs, down to the complication of the groin, the legs, the clenched toes.

The Doktor grin-winces. The prosthesis jiggles and gleams. He remarks in an even tone, 'I expect you're like all my other disciples. You will purport to quote my exact words, but you will misinterpret me.'

'I'll do my best, actually.'

'I'm not wrong. Never.'

'Never?'

'Never! . . . Never, never,' he whispers.

'You're as great as Shakespeare,' Jones concedes.

'I dismiss you!'

Under normal circumstances it would be inadvisable to give more morphine so soon – however . . . Jones draws another 5 cc into the syringe. He raises The Doktor's left arm and rests it on the rim of the tub and pats the inside of the elbow with an alcohol-soaked swab, and there, into the vein, the needle goes. The Doktor gasps. Soon once again he has become dreamy, hard to understand, communicating in no known language, between sleep and wakefulness.

Quetzal

Silence continues.

In silence, The Doktor waits.

He stands behind the head of the couch, listening.

The patient is stretched out, prone (asleep? no, awake, certainly) and silent.

The Doktor attends to silence. Silently, he gazes down at the patient's eyelashes, the pores in the patient's nose . . . and across at a Hellenic bust: the goddess of wisdom, Athena, being born from Zeus' head.

The allotted fifty-five minutes is up.

The patient pays the fee (seven guineas) and departs – in silence.

Five minutes' worth of silence ensues. It is The Doktor's due. His respite.

The Doktor is a connoisseur of silences. Silence occurs

often during his sessions – and often for the whole of it; more and more patients, it seems, are feeling the need to say nothing. Just as many artists have painted a plain white canvas, some many times, and each painting has a specific connotation – so every psychoanalytic silence cries out for individualized interpretation.

There is the silence which is a beginning, and the silence which is an end. The silence which is led up to, and the silence which leads away from. The silence of intermission: the *in medias res* silence. The silence that blocks; the silence that releases. The silence that is eternal; the silence that is a blink of the eye; the silence that takes what it takes. Happy silence; miserable silence; neither-nor silence. Self-satisfied silence; self-doubting silence; self-mocking silence. Sympathetic silence; antagonistic silence; the silence that is a negotiating tactic. The silence that is the articulation of non-silences; the silence that *is* a non-silence; the noise that is, really, a kind of silence. 'Abreactive' silence which is a kind of diverted hysteria. The silence of a hypnotic trance-like state. The silence of 'transference' when the patient falls in love with The Doktor; the silence of . . . (but no: The Doktor never falls in love with the patient). Unclassifiable silences.

And this is as it should be. For The Doktor is living (he understands) in a City of Silence. Or at least, if not yet, this shall soon come to pass. The city is being emptied. Children are being sent away, just in case, to Canada or the United States, Australia or New Zealand, or even to second cousins in Lanarkshire . . . as far away as possible from where the bombs are, conceivably, going to drop; and not-very-secret plans are being drawn up to relocate whole schools, en masse, to the provinces. Old Masters from the National Gallery are sneaking off to a disused Welsh coal mine. The animals in the Regent's Park zoo are being packed off to Whipsnade, their rural retreat, for the duration. To minimize alarm to the public, the big cats are jaunting incognito in unmarked vehicles – but all too many pedestrians, paused at the traffic lights opposite the World's End pub, have sniffed mysterious tawny odours emanating from within an alleged Sunpride bakery van. A gorilla was spied lounging at the back of a taxi in Maresfield Gardens. Somebody late one night on Prince Albert Road sighted a zebra crossing a zebra-crossing. They say the elephants will be next; then the camels; the wolves not far behind. The exotic birds will be distant as the idea of birds. The giraffes, though, those most silent and unpackable of creatures, will be left till last.

The food is becoming tasteless. Flowers odourless. The weather is neither hot nor cold, wet nor dry. Conversations might as well be silent for all that the words mean. When the wireless is switched on, as often as not only interference is to be heard. We that are left (The Doktor thinks), those of us not in the army nor the countryside nor about to flee anywhere further, we walk around with evacuated heads, our minds elsewhere.

Reality

Imagine a city where there is no private mental experience. Or rather, it may exist, but there is no way of expressing the concept, no vocabulary for it. Of what we cannot speak, thereof we cannot even whistle. For example: this man may be tall, this woman fat, but he cannot be 'wishful' nor she 'homesick' – such words are meaningless. The political situation may well be 'sad' – but not an individual. A solicitor chances to run across the very barrister he has been trying to get hold of all week – in, of all places, the Pig and Whistle in Fitzroy Square, during a darts contest: this may justly be called a 'happy coincidence', but it would be impertinent to describe either lawyer as 'happy'. General practitioners are troubled by a host of patients with vague symptoms, of a kind we might name 'nostalgia', say, or 'joy'. The physician takes the pulse, the temperature, the blood pressure, checks the urine and the stool, inquires about sleep and regularity of the bowels. The patient is prescribed a couple of aspirin and a hot water bottle. Quite often this does the trick. A successful stockbroker, taking the Northern Line underground train en route from his Hampstead home to his office in Shoreditch, finds himself seated opposite a queerly familiar figure – a chap, now red-faced and balding, hunched, in a patched tweed suit, who had bullied him throughout his years at preparatory school. What emotions assail the stockbroker? Does he feel hatred; desire for revenge; triumph; forgiveness; curiosity? No, none of the above, of course. The stockbroker clears his throat. He gently taps the ferrule of his umbrella on the floor. He remarks, 'Good morning, Lloyd-Jones. Long time no see.'

Is madness possible in such a city? Of course; but it is not to be characterized thus. If an 'agoraphobic' (as we could call him) refuses to venture out through the front door of his Eton Avenue maisonette, it is concluded that, for example, a freak storm is liable to break out, one of those rare August tempests with much crackly lightning; or that, say, the plaster cornices along the street are fragile and might topple: best to wear a stout hat at all times. That woman who 'obsessively' washes her hands until they are raw – her behaviour is evidence that the city is full of dangerous germs: prudent citizens would be wise to copy her. The 'paranoid' who asserts dangerous ruffians are on the loose, conspiring to murder their victims for the most arbitrary of reasons – his claim may be rejected or accepted, but, such as it is, it refers not to one psyche but to the city, the world.

And even the (as we would say) 'insane' people themselves, they project their feelings externally. The manic-depressive, when in the manic state, seeks out the Court News in the paper, and delights in the information that, say, Princess Elizabeth has been taking her favourite Shetland pony for a jolly long ride in Hyde Park. When depressed he reads the news from overseas.

As for lovers, to them it is an objective fact that his earlobes possess a peculiar charm; that there is glamour in her eyelashes; that Bonzo (his Yorkshire terrier) is the most delightful dog that ever could be; that Sans Souci, Netherhall Gardens (where she, the beloved, resides) is the most beautiful house in creation; that the whole city (ah! those granite kerbs; oho! the number 28 bus to West Hampstead; hey-hey! the nimbo-cumulus formation) is wonderful and rich and strange. And if others disagree, then they are mistaken.

Poets are public spokesmen, or else they are frauds.

Painters are essentially narrators.

Psychoanalysts are . . . But no, there are no psychoanalysts here; or, if there are, they are irredeemably bearded, unnaturally foreign; associated with a bygone era – to be ignored.

Yet, even in this city, there are some eccentrics who seek a private self; they suspect, contrary to the orthodoxy, they are each, in some way, special: that there are sensations and ideas only the individual has access to. They are impelled, then – since no vocabulary pre-exists, and it would be absurd to apply collective adjectives such as 'merry' or 'fearful' to oneself – to invent their own. For example: 'I'm fwibbly,' they might utter in their heads (corresponding to our 'curious'); or they might tell themselves, 'I am undergoing swobbleclitch,' (that state of rasped-clean mental clarity, following the acceptance of a disaster); or, 'I'm quatt,' (meaning who-knows-what). But within that category of deviants, the ones, the only ones, who are prepared to admit and announce their mental states, they are children. The grown-ups laugh at the girl's hubristic folly, the boy's egoism . . . The children will grow older, and forget.

Sleep

The Doktor, taking a pre-lunch nap on his own couch, with the Collected Works of Shakespeare Volume VI (*Julius Caesar* to *Antony and Cleopatra*) tucked under his head in place of a pillow, is woken by a distinctive woof-woof. So startled is he that he rolls off – but makes a soft landing on the oriental carpet, settling on hands and feet. He inhales the dust. His sneeze, held back for some seconds, escapes in a breathy roar – composite names – Ptah/Thoth/Horus/Ra . . .

What confronts him, when he rises and leans for stability's sake against his mantelpiece, is a row of small jasper and basalt statuettes (looted from an Eighteenth Dynasty tomb in the Valley of the Kings by a professional mummy-thief and subsequently sold to a camp follower of Napoleon . . . and acquired by its present owner during the period of his medical studies in Paris half a century ago from an antiquities dealer in the rue du Dragon):

representations of those good old gods. The one directly under his nose is the dog-headed Anubis, whose job it was to conduct the dead to their judgment: to the Ceremony of the Weighing of the Heart.

Nevertheless The Doktor is not in an Ancient Egyptian afterlife – for the psychopomp's muzzled head is plainly a carved mineral. Yet the noise continues. The Doktor recognizes it: it is the familiar bark of his own pet chow. The chow is not to be seen: it must be recessed somewhere within the building.

And, naturally, the chow is answered by the collie that belongs to the occupants of the adjoining house. Some echo effect – an acoustical oddity – serves to amplify its call, as if that dog too were inside this very room. In turn, the collie is challenged by the wolfhound at number 32 – its snarl also resounds across the consulting room. And soon all the dogs of Maresfield Gardens – number 18's chihuahua; the Welsh terrier of the Goldschmidts at number 41; the saluki that occupies number 5's garage; the Smith-Klein (number 12's) pair of racing whippets . . . respond with their own respective yip and howl and wuff and grrr-grrr.

The Doktor steadies himself, and goes to the front door. He wipes his carpet slippers on the Welcome mat. He steps out on the brick porch. To his unsurprise a convocation of dogs is taking place. Not merely the local neighbourhood dogs, but others, who must have scampered here from more distant suburbs – beagle of West Hampstead and Fortune Green bloodhound, Child's Hill's own husky and the Shih-Tzu from St John's Wood – are sounding off and cavorting and fighting, in their various manners, up and down the street.

A dachshund puppy is dodging behind The Doktor's ankles, taking shelter – and he recalls the sad history of that breed. Condemned on account of their Germanic name, the dachshunds of England were put to sleep en masse during the late summer of 1914; it's a dog's life. (The poodles, oddly, though etymologically just as Boche, managed to 'pass' and were tolerated. The German shepherd dogs were renamed Alsatians, and hailed as loyal allies.)

Yes, The Doktor is in the city of the dogs. It consists notably of kennels, constructed by prominent architects in mock-Tudor, for instance, or Art Deco 'Assyrian' style; the kennel by the crossroads where Maresfield Gardens cuts into Nutley Terrace, that one is a splendid example of High Gothic, comparable in terms of technique and moral seriousness with the Albert Memorial in Hyde Park. The kennels are not numbered, but are known by the nameplates hammered into their pediments: Growler's, Chez Bow-Wow, My Bone . . .

Of course habitations for humans exist alongside, as a

rule associated with a particular kennel – but these are mere workaday annexes, about which little need be said.

The humans, such as they are, are seldom seen in public except when tugged along by their dominant animal: the leash is wrapped tight around the person's wrist. And it is rare for people to interact until and unless their dogs have done so first: only as a coda to a mutual sniff, tussle, leash-entanglement, might a pair of accompanists exchange a remark on the weather or politics or how nice somebody's coiffure is looking. In fact the humans of Maresfield Gardens, who maintain a decent formality, know each other mostly in terms of their dogs. 'Isn't she the borzoi?' one asks. 'I do believe he is the Yorkshire terrier.'

For the most part humans are bigger than dogs, and almost as loud, and more numerous; and the houses and buildings that serve humans are grander and commoner than those for dogs. Notwithstanding this is the city of dogs. (The human is the dog's best friend.) Notwithstanding.

For – and this is the essence of it – it is believed that human thought is, at best, a rough draft of dog psychology. Dogs (it is said) are faithful, and direct, and live for the moment: they love and hate freely; they have no sense of mortality and so are liberated from it. Humans aspire to these conditions, which they would achieve if only they could rid themselves of the petty twists and complexes, the repressions and sublimations which so torture them. The task of psychoanalysis, then, is to render the subject more dog-like.

The Doktor has been noticing changes in that direction. If men do not yet deposit smellmarks to bound their terrain, and sniff their females' behinds, and bury their valuables in public spaces only to forget where they had been hidden and be thereby impelled to create a thousand holes . . . it seems not impossible they will soon do something along those lines.

The Doktor goes inside again and drags the door shut.

He gulps cold air.

His tongue lolls.

From memory, silently, he recites a prayer from The Book of the Dead. *O heart of my mother, O heart of my mother, O my heart of my coming into being, do not stand up against me as a witness before the Guardian of the Balance.*

He can count the faltering drumbeat of his own pulse.

The Doktor totters forward, into the consulting room, across the carpet's fringed edge.

The next patient is already inside, rampant on the couch – muzzle bared, tail erect.

Teacher

The mistress, to draw her class into the appropriate mood, is reading aloud a poem written by one of the combatants of the Great War. It concerns a gas attack. *'If you had seen . . .'* the mistress quotes. She evokes the greenish-yellowish fumes drifting and billowing across no-man's-land, the trenches; the soldiers coughing their lungs out. The children listen in silence, only mildly bored. *'If you had seen . . .'* the children echo, as required. Shafts of sunshine, milky with chalk dust, descend diagonally. A bluebottle buzzes.

Next, obeying instructions, the pupils rummage in their canvas sacks, each indelibly inked with a family name plus an initial to minimize confusion, to extract their gas masks. One child's sack is embroidered with Winnie-the-Pooh. The mistress fits on her own mask. The explanation continues – her voice is now metamorphosed to a babble, incomprehensible. A half-hearted giggle from a child, or two. The insect settles on a pane; is silent. The class also is silent, rapt, absorbed in the mistress's no-speech. The children understand enough to know they too must put on theirs. Consider a classroom containing only rows of windowpanes; rows of electric ceiling lamps; rows of desks with inkwells and nib pens; rows of chairs; seated creatures with the bodies of children and, in place of heads, a mechanico-bestial apparatus; a dead bluebottle; a masked mistress chalking an isosceles triangle on the blackboard. How can one prove that the angles on opposite sides are equal?

Along Gloucester Avenue, a youngish man in a newish suit is walking. He is rapping door knockers and pressing electric bells. Under his arm he carries a sheaf of brochures, glossy and bright with three-colour printing: these he displays to dedicated housewives and concerned mothers, to devoted husbands and considerate fathers; they incorporate pictures of his company's plots and stones and urns and weeping angels – a price list is discreetly inserted at the back. The fashion, these days, is for something simple yet impressive: let's say a shiny block of jet with gilt trimmings, the name and dates carved deep. This salesman has good taste. He wouldn't so much as dream of lifting the lion-head door knocker of a home where somebody is sick or dying, or even excessively elderly (he has an intuition for such things: he can always tell); besides – contrary to what you might imagine – that is not where the good customers are. Young marrieds are indeed the best prospects. For how better to celebrate the present than to contemplate its transience?

And now that the city itself faces the prospect of destruction: while the air-raid sirens blow (just testing!) and all rush down to the shelters (time is consumed in the playing of board games, in reading magazines dedicated to True Life crimes ('My Husband Dropped Rat Poison In My Kedgeree!') and cuddling intimately, chastely, under the blankets), the mundane is granted value and beauty. Even the ugly may seem attractive: those Art Deco lumpish office buildings, their entablatures distended as shot-putters' shoulders, those cheap brick rectangular homes . . . just close your eyes and envision them bombed, torn, cracked open, a scrap of damp charred wallpaper flopping like an old carp's loose skin. How precious their current existence is.

These thoughts pass through the Valuer's head. His job, after all, is to assign an estimate to objects – so that this should be known in the event that they should cease to be. Lately he has had his work cut out for him. Under the circumstances, so many owners are making sure their insurance policy is up to date, so many wills are being written. Of course nothing in this world has an exact value:

some owners would like to be told a high figure, to match their own self-estimate, others prefer something on the low side, for Inheritance Tax reasons, perhaps.

The Valuer is pacing gradually around the consulting room at number 20 Maresfield Gardens, pausing to pencil in prices against the list of items on his inventory. He sighs. 'I'm afraid there's not much demand these days for your assortment of ancient gods,' he informs the aged refugee slumped in a rattan rocking chair. 'Let's say a hundred guineas for the case of little ones. Of course we'll have to add on sixty extra for your Athena and your Buddha, and there's always a fair demand for Sphinxes. Your Anubis, too, is in pretty good condition.'

The Doktor smiles and nods. He seems pleased – whether at the thought of the low price or the fine condition is unclear.

The Valuer is now peering at a sketch, a portrait of the old man by an artist who signs himself Dali. Shoddy draughtsmanship, the Valuer thinks; of purely sentimental value. Whereas this souvenir mountainscape from Bad Gastein – now that might be worth a few bob.

But at last the Valuer is struck by a truly exciting antique, a remarkable specimen indeed. It is a model ship in a bottle, a sailing ship, ingeniously and skilfully carved out of dyed limewood, the rigging is utterly decorative and inauthentic.

(How was it fitted inside the narrow-necked bottle? Aha, the sails were erected after the insertion, by means of a secret string.) The bottle is reposed on an ebony stand, inscribed with what the Valuer identifies as the motto of the Hanseatic League: *Navigare necesse est, vivere non necesse.* 'To sail is necessary, to live is not necessary.' Which gives him a clue as to its origin and probable date.

Like a professional Memory Man at the music hall, or a psychoanalyst with a patient, the Valuer is obliged to give an impression of serious thinking. He crouches. He tilts his head this way and that. He sucks through his teeth.

'Continental Victoriana,' he informs the refugee at last. 'From Germany or Austro-Hungary.'

The Doktor grins; insists, 'I made it myself, when I was a child.'

Naturally the Valuer refuses to listen. (Owners have such strange ideas about their property!) 'An important and highly collectable item.'

The Doktor repeats: 'No, no.'

The Valuer ignores the outburst. 'I've come across a comparable work in a Sotheby's sale, but not in such good condition. Who knows what this could fetch at auction?'

The Doktor shakes his head and indeed much of his body, as if wrestling with a demon. The rocking chair swings and squirms. He groans, '*Nein!*'

The Valuer stares hard at the crumpled figure of the old man. The twisted greyish skin. The mouse-eaten beard. The bright, bloodshot eyes. The Valuer states in a low voice, scarcely bothering to make himself heard: 'Not historically accurate and not beautiful but all the same . . . it is a rare and precious example of nineteenth-century naive art.'

Unbedenklichkeitserklärung

Spot the nine hundred and ninety-nine deliberate mistakes. It is morning. The greengrocer is cranking down the awning over his shop, using the special long hooked pole. The sweetshop owner is arranging his humbugs, his nonpareils, his swarthy strands of liquorice, the banknotes in his till. A dustman, on his day off, goes shopping for a wedding ring. The blackbirds are singing sweetly on all the houses. Yet there is more to this than meets the eye. The greengrocer is in love with a butcher's wife who loves a policeman. The sweetshop owner has been informed he has inoperable cancer of the pancreas. The dustman has got a nursery school teacher into trouble; he is wondering if he should run away and join the army, or possibly the navy, the air force, or pursue a business opportunity in non-ferrous metals (wholesale). The blackbirds keep singing on the gutters and drainpipes and upper-floor balconies and soot-stained red-tiled roofs, sweetly. And at 28 Akenside Road, in the sitting room in Flat 19B, a white-haired woman is absolutely still. She is propped up in an armchair. She has been absolutely still since March 1922. Her daughters tend her; comb her, feed her, see to her sanitary needs. She has become quite plump. Also, less than half a mile away at 48 Gloucester Avenue, a dentist whose wife has left him cries in his office. She eloped with the milkman from Express Dairies: they rode away on the horse-drawn cart, they and the crates of used empties, to their love nest in Kentish Town. Hence the dentist is distraught, self-pitying, pitiful: what can all his expertise in dentistry do for him now? Of what use is his tooth-pulling apparatus; his framed diploma; his ether; his specialized knowledge of caries; his stock of gold amalgam; his filing cabinet filled with dental records? Similarly, a mile to the north, in Hampstead, a novelist is afflicted. He has locked himself in his study at 54 Willoughby Road, together with his Crown-Archer type-writer and his stack of bond paper, and refuses to come out. He has published four comedies of manners about the idiosyncrasies of contemporary life, the latest one a decided *succès d'estime*; yet now he is blocked. It is absurd: it is intolerable: he has never been blocked before; his wife weeps and and his children batter on the door, 'Please, Daddy, come down to breakfast, your porridge is becoming lumpy,' but he refuses to emerge. He glares at the blank sheet.

In due course, as the morning wears on, the catatonic's eldest daughter telephones a certain number. Which is also rung by the cuckolded dentist. Also by the novelist's wife. Appointments are made for that very afternoon . . .

For this is a city in which psychiatry, sometimes, actually, is just the ticket.

At one o'clock, The Doktor pays a house call on the catatonic. He turns up at 28 Akenside Road. He presses the appropriate spot on the bell push. The middle daughter opens the door, and beckons him through and up to Flat 19B. A musty place, tidied up a little in preparation for his visit, but still none too perfect. The Axminster is frayed. The wallpaper has an old-fashioned peony pattern. The Doktor wastes no time. He takes out his gold fob watch, and swings it by its chain in front of the catatonic's eyes. Soon she is hypnotized. In a trance state, she goes back to that terrible day in 1922, in her girlhood, when she was sunk into inaction. She recalls being sexually abused by a chimney sweep. Now that she has brought into the forefront of her consciousness this dark secret, she is free to exorcise it. 'It's not your fault. You are not to blame,' she tells herself. For it is a tenet of psychoanalysis that once one understands the original trauma, one is liberated from it. 'Previous philosophers have interpreted the world, my task is to change it,' as The Doktor seems to remember having written in one of his many tomes. Also: 'If you will it, it is no dream.' The upshot is that the catatonic is completely cured. Hands are shaken all round. The Doktor is paid his fee by the youngest daughter. He turns down the offer of a shot of Famous Grouse; makes his own way out, waves down a taxi, and goes home. Meanwhile the ex-catatonic takes her daughters on a shopping expedition to John Barnes department store, near Swiss Cottage; she makes a beeline for a set of pillowcases in best Belfast linen, a standard lamp with a maroon shade, and an amusing tea cosy shaped like Big Ben.

The tearful dentist arrives at two o'clock. He is ushered in. He lies down on the couch. The Doktor stands behind him. The analyst is, of course, silent. Silence prevails for a good five minutes or so. Then, spontaneously, the dentist recalls his earliest memory of his childhood; his relationship with his domineering father; he discovers his latent algolagnic leaning which he has long sublimated in his dentistry. Knowing himself truly, for the first time in his life, he is reconciled to his fate. He is determined to dedicate the rest of his life to his work; furthermore he has long had his eye on one of his patients, an accommodating widow: he will definitely pop the question. He thanks the psychoanalyst, and departs. Another success for The Doktor.

By the time the blocked novelist arrives, at three, The Doktor has arranged his Rorschach tests on the desk. A selection of choice inkblots. The novelist describes what he sees in each. This leads him to realize that, as he is the first to confess, 'While on the one hand I must cultivate my super-ego, it must not hog the limelight, and by stifling my id, at the same time as giving my ego full rein, I have smothered my creative juices. Now, thanks to you and your wonderful psychoanalysis, Doktor, I have achieved an appropriate balance. Furthermore I have plenty of ideas for a new comedy of manners. I shall rush home and type up page one.'

Hard to believe in this city, yes; but harder still to disbelieve in it. Why should psychoanalysis not, at least twice or thrice, work? There may be failures; there may be analyses that drag on for years; there may be courses of treatment that end in X's terminal depression, in Y's suicide; but surely, on some occasions, for some patients, in some city (why not this one?) The Doktor's methods will triumph.

It is the morning, again.

It is the morning, still.

The Doktor is taking his daily constitutional down Finchley Road. (Whether he is any position to do so is not the point: the question is whether it is conceivable.) The ferrule of his bamboo walking stick bangs wildly on the pavement. He is in pain; his palatal prosthesis gives him no surcease. Yet he twists his head round to look at the city – the parallel strands of telegraph wire like the rulings on music paper; the pollarded plane trees; the Continental delicatessen where the refugees buy their salami; the beer shop; the greengrocer's; the steep roofs the colour of dried blood . . . could this be the city where mental suffering is temporary; where distress is more than understandable: it may be excised; where anybody who bothers to lie down on the couch of a competent analyst stands a decent chance of attaining peace of mind, a satisfied life . . . could this be that city: this city here: here . . . here where blackbirds sing so sweetly?

'How are you?'

There is no reply.

Sunshine is scarce in the consulting room. The blackout curtains are half-drawn and the looking glasses have been placed flat against the wall. The Doktor is enthroned in the armchair, staring out into nowhere.

'More morphine?'

The Doktor sighs. 'You well know I never take any opiate.'

'No?'

'I refuse to let my mind be dulled.'

'Is that so?'

'Possibly I might accept a little aspirin.'

Jones opens his black bag. He rolls up The Doktor's left sleeve.

'We shall have to get somebody in to mow the lawn,' the Doktor observes. 'And the hollyhocks, they need lopping.'

'But you're looking at the secretaire. The antiques . . .'

'Who?'

'I said: this is Anubis . . . Hermes . . . a wine jar . . . a syringe containing a tenth of a grain of morphia, just sufficient to take the edge off the pain . . . Horus . . . a Bodhisattva . . .

'More,' The Doktor murmurs.

'. . . a canopic urn . . . Aphrodite . . . Osiris . . .'

'Aha, I know him well. I purchased him at Lustig's on Wieblingerstrasse. After his death he was resurrected, and he became King of the Afterlife.'

'Really?' Jones says, as he injects the painkiller.

At four o'clock the cuckoo clock sounds off.

Silence follows.

'Was that an air-raid siren?' The Doktor mumbles.

The Doktor mouths the long vowel of 'chow'.

'In the corner,' Jones says. 'I do believe it is distressed by the odour from your necrosis.'

The Doktor tries to turn his head.

'It is scrabbling against the French windows.'

The Doktor's mouth bends in a kind of grin.

'*Wanderlust.*'

The Doktor's groans and panting become worse. An hour later, at approximately 5.30 p.m., Jones injects another tenth of a grain of morphia, in combination with caffeine, calcium, digitalis.

The Doktor seems asleep. But then he utters a remark, in a normal enough voice.

'This city. London. Is it of interest?'

'Not bad.'

'I must visit it some time.'

Six-ten p.m. Jones wipes down The Doktor's face with a damp flannel, paying special attention to the corners of the eyes and nostrils. This seems to give some relief. Half a grain of morphia, intravenously.

'Do you want to hear a good joke?' says The Doktor.

At 7.22 p.m. The Doktor commences the joke.

'The Great Rabbi of Minsk was in the synagogue, surrounded by all his followers – when suddenly he waved his hands in the air and shouted, "I have a vision! The Great Rabbi of Pinsk has died! We must all go into mourning!"'

The Doktor experiences a violent pain in the vicinity of the buccal mucous membrane, and is unable to continue with the amusing story.

The joke recommences at 7.37 p.m.

'So the Great Rabbi of Minsk and all his followers went into mourning. And they stayed in mourning for several days . . .'

The joke breaks off.

Jones stands behind The Doktor, his arms around the old man's shoulders, his thumbs inside the mouth, adjusting the prosthesis.

At 7.44 p.m. Jones whispers:

'Go on. Tell me. They had all been in mourning for several days, and then . . .?'

'Then a visitor arrived in Minsk from Pinsk. And he told the Great Rabbi of Minsk: "I saw the Great Rabbi of Pinsk just yesterday, and he is in perfectly fine health."'

'He is in perfectly fine health. Yes? And then what?'

Severe repeated pains at the nasal-palatal border necessitate a further half grain of morpia at 7.58 p.m.

Remarkably, by 8.02 p.m. The Doktor has recovered sufficiently to continue:

'The Great Rabbi of Minsk and all his followers ceased their mourning. With what joy they celebrated the resurrection of the Great Rabbi of Pinsk.'

But then problems with the prosthesis make The Doktor's speech unintelligible, the joke seemingly pointless.

The Doktor is scarcely conscious.

However at 8.22 p.m. The Doktor's shoulders and jaw twist and shudder repeatedly, as if trying to escape from Houdini-bonds, as if trying to bite through his own mouth.

And Jones feels called upon to carry out what The Doktor, were he in a position to do so, would demand . . . Or so Jones convinces himself.

He draws into the syringe ten grains of morphia in 7 per cent solution.

He holds The Doktor's right hand upturned on his own, and wipes the wrist with an alcohol-soaked swab – though really there is no point in this precaution, under the circumstances. He slides the needle into the wrist vein: pushes the plunger down.

Jones tugs The Doktor's fob watch from its pocket. He verifies this time on his own wristwatch, and on the mantel clock.

It is 8.31 p.m. He estimates the procedure will take twenty minutes until completion.

At 8.41 p.m. Jones withdraws a Romeo y Julieta cigar from the box on the secretaire. He cuts off the tip with a scalpel. He makes use of The Doktor's platinum lighter – engraved to the effect that it was donated by a grateful person or organization, on some occasion or another.

The Doktor's cigar is between Jones's lips. He is taking one long deep satisfying puff.

At 8.45 p.m. he takes the cigar from his own mouth and sets it in The Doktor's. He twists it into place, squeezing it between the lower incisors and the palatal prosthesis. The cigar glows steadily: offers up its rich aroma and drops its ash. Smoke enters and – passing through the incision in the prosthesis – emerges from the nostrils as a pair of smoke-horns. Soon smoke encircles The Doktor's head – a cloud of smoke.

Jones takes the pulse.

At 9.00 p.m. the cuckoo clock performs.

Jones dutifully feeds the chow and waters the house plants.

But at 9.10 p.m. the cigar is still burning gradually down, and the pulse is steady.

Though it seems scarcely likely that The Doktor could revive, given the quantum of morphine, the prospect is intolerable. How dare he?

Jones extracts the cigar from The Doktor's mouth. He grinds the stub down in an ashtray – a Hellenic krater decorated with a red-figure Dionysiac design.

He crouches to lower himself to the requisite height, and putting his left hand behind the neck and the right on the small of the back, levers the old man up. The body is lighter and more manoeuvrable than might be thought, light as a girl's.

Jones, stepping out alternately right and left, swaying to and fro, lifts the body, shifts it, up from the armchair, over the carpet, ever closer to the couch, as if, for all the world, he were dancing with The Doktor . . .

Now The Doktor is supine, in the posture of any of his own patients.

Jones tilts the cool forehead.

The mouth jerks open, revealing the dingy-shiny prosthesis.

Jones reaches out for the nearest object to hand – what appears to have slipped behind the couch – a first edition of *The Interpretation of Dreams*, translated by himself – and going down on both knees so that his head is at the level of The Doktor's, hugs him close, places and presses the open book down firmly over The Doktor's mouth and nostrils; the face is covered.

And so Jones never gets to hear the end of it.

But this is of no account – since he has heard the story before – he has heard all The Doktor's stories before. He knows them by heart.

Jones narrates the punch line. Silently.

'. . . The visitor from Pinsk remarked to one of the Great Rabbi of Minsk's followers, "Your Great Rabbi was wrong, wasn't he?"'

'And the follower replied, "Ah, but even so, to see all the way from Minsk to Pinsk – now wasn't that a magnificent achievement!"'

Valhalla

Blue eyes have run out at Madame Tussaud's. The sole supplier was a Bohemian glassworks: ever since the Sudetenland fell, it has only been a matter of time. For some months now the management has been adopting the stopgap policy of manufacturing only duskier dummies, Semitic or Mediterranean types plus the odd Oriental and Negro – at any rate those with irises of some shade of brown or grey.

The Doktor, notably. (His gaze changes hue depending on the ambient light – but is dark, always dark.) A month or several months ago he was photographed and sketched; he donated little-worn garments; he has finally received an invitation to view himself . . . And here he is, leaning on his walking stick, inspecting the imitation.

This is not how he had envisaged it. He had supposed he would be present at a grand ceremony. An inauguration. An unveiling. There would be speeches. Certainly there would be speeches! There would be toasts. There would be applause. Applause aplenty! A standing ovation. And, at the climax . . .

But enough of daydreaming. No doubt sloe-eyed dummies have been installed lately; dozens of them. No doubt, in terms of drawing power, he is far from the most important dummy present (he eavesdrops on a pair of puzzled housewives: 'Is that the axe-murderer?' 'No, dear, he's the other one' – as they slope off down the hall) which is only to be expected; and should be welcomed.

He assesses his twin. This fake has a trimmer, browner beard than in reality; fewer lines on the forehead; the long asymmetric wrinkles between the corners of its mouth and eyes: these are implausibly gentle; far from sharing his own solemn official mien, the dummy actually smiles! It is wearing a velvet-lapelled smoking jacket, polka-dot four-in-hand bow tie, boldly striped trousers – an outfit he would never be in the mood for these days. No, this dummy looks fitter and more at peace than he has been since before the first symptoms of . . . since the death of . . . before the Great War, at least.

So inexact is this imitation that no passer-by seems to remark the resemblance. He had supposed boys would gaze at himself and itself, and giggle; that, if he had stood still too long, his earlobe might be pinched, as a test; that an inquisitive person would plunge an uncoiled safety-pin into his cheek . . . Really, Tussaud's reputation for exactitude is unjustified: so The Doktor concludes.

Well, obviously he had misapprehended this city. He had supposed the English were a stiff, upright people, holding themselves separate from their own bodies, valuing them only as machines rather inferior to sound horseflesh (a mistake derived from reading the works of R. L. Stevenson and Mary Shelley). On the basis of his experience of certain Continental waxworks he had presumed dummies neatly arranged in a row: one would be led past by a guide muttering in hushed tones: one would admire the illustrious fakes; one might curtsey, or click one's heels and jerk an arm out.

Not a bit of it! The viewers drift at random; they slouch and slump. The dummy is to be admired as a token of the real one, its ambassador, so its precise appearance really isn't the point. Which is disappointing and reassuring.

He is reminded of the quintessential Viennese dinner-party pastime: the manufacture of *Gschnas*. How many Psychoanalytical Congresses ago was it that he and Ferenczi and Jung and Jones had collaborated on putting together a knight in armour out of bread rolls, a candlestick, a dish of chopped liver and a set of silver toothpicks? Then he and his colleagues had outdone themselves; they had made a Torah scroll out of little more than an apfelstrudel and a couple of Frau F—'s sanitary napkins.

The Doktor-dummy stands in a consulting room – a corner of a consulting room, rather – containing a couch which is stubbier than his true one, less protrusive, draped with an unspecial Axminster, beside a desk on which are some reproductions of Horus, Mut, Jupiter . . . a pigskin-bound volume or three of *Judisches Lexikon* . . . oblique references to the true room, at best.

As The Doktor waits, some figures do eventually float over to his doppelgänger. An androgynous fellow in an Inverness cape. A woman, pregnant, who keeps toying with a ring on the fourth finger of her left hand. A young clerk, carbuncular . . . And these, all these, they are talking to themselves. They do not actually lie down on the couch, since it is cordoned off by a rope and a NO ENTRY sign. But they stand fairly still, not far from the dummy, and respond to its silence.

Yes, the dummy is superbly silent. As effective a psychoanalyst, perhaps, as The Doktor himself.

He is dismayed; then comforted; then dismayed. That he should be offered *this* afterlife . . .

Well, so be it. He takes a slow stroll down the hall. He makes the acquaintance of the fellow-residents of this establishment. Kings. Playwrights. Scientists. Gangsters. Lunatics.

Millionaires . . . and is not surprised to discover, in the vicinity of other eminent dummies, the occasional troubled visitor whispering. Her secret lust is confided to Queen Victoria; his true desire to Napoleon; her grief to Mae West; his earliest childhood memory is for Charlie Chaplin's ears alone . . .

In a backroom at Madame Tussaud's, the Chief Imitatress is carrying out the desperate measures these desperate times demand. Using a sharpened warmed teaspoon she is extracting blue eyeballs from lesser aristocrats guillotined during the Terror, and inserting them into Winston Churchill (complete with authentic cigar) and Princess Elizabeth on her azure-eyed Shetland pony.

W*ater*

A schoolgirl is riding down Primrose Hill Road on her dappled gelding. The day is bright. She lifts her right hand in a salute posture to shade her eyes. For a strange sight has caught her notice. On the road not so far ahead, where it rises in a little fold then dips again, is a pool of water. It is glimmering in the sunshine. 'Come on, old chap,' she murmurs in her gelding's ear. The beast tosses its head and neighs; then, obedient, canters downhill . . . But when they arrive at the supposed pool there is nothing but dry tarmacadam! 'Oh golly gosh,' the girl says. She rides round up the hill again, and cuts across the park to the bathtub-shaped trough on Gloucester Avenue – where the gelding drinks his fill, while the schoolgirl stands beside him, stroking his mane and muttering, 'There, there.'

Similarly, a brush salesman is knocking on the doors of the houses along Elsworthy Road and inquiring, 'Excuse me, madam. Would it be all right if I dropped ash on your carpet and swept it up with my amazing new appliance?' – getting the usual percentage of rejections and doors slammed in his face, but chalking up a victory from time to time . . . when what should he see, hovering in midair directly above where number 73 used to stand before it was burned down as an insurance fraud, but the House of Commons, somewhat reduced in size, upside down? A portion of Big Ben is also included. The vision is a little hazy, even at the start, and within half an hour or so fades into a glowing mist. The salesman raps on the door of number 75, holding his patent carpet brush before him as proof of his honest intentions.

For mirages pop up quite often in and around this city – especially in the northern and northwestern suburbs. You could hardly say they are an everyday occurrence, but they are frequent enough not to be worth making an excessive fuss over. The physics of them is well understood by those who care about that kind of thing – an illusion due to light refracted and bent back on itself by successive layers of heated air. If you should chance to see one, it would not be out of order to mention the matter in the pub that evening, but it is no proof of your special election: you cannot reasonably expect to dine out on the story for months.

Nevertheless, the inhabitants of the city are (or, at least, used to be, in the old days) quite proud of their mirages, and take an interest in their wellbeing. In the spring of 1932, the London County Council established a Committee For The Amelioration Of The Urban Mirage. The fundamental problem they ran up against, however, is that the mirage is not a reliable animal. It comes and it goes. You can entice a charabanc full of Sunday School attendees up Parliament Hill to view the wonder – but, likely as not, there will be nothing to be seen.

So the Mirage Committee, after much cogitation and consideration of various practical and impractical suggestions, declared itself in favour of the imposition of an Artifical Mirage to be erected in the southwest corner of Regent's Park – not too far away from Madame Tussaud's and the Planetarium. The Mirage would be year round, independent of climatic conditions (it would operate even during drizzle, or in the severest fog) and would be at once amusing and educational.

It was built by a firm of theatrical suppliers, promptly. It opened in July of the following year. It was, by all accounts, a technological marvel. In the very first week, thousands of sightseers gawped at the wonder – a vision of central London hovering, inverted, over a grass field in the north of it. Some sharp-eyed children saw remarkable sights in it.

'Oh look, there's my Daddy, kissing a funny lady with very red lips,' – or so the rumours went. Implausible, actually – it was never as clear (mirages never are, you know) as it was supposed to be.

For several months it was quite a draw. To visit London without seeing the Artificial Mirage seemed as absurd as, say, going all the way to India without getting around to potting a tiger, or leaving Switzerland never having dunked a crust into molten cheese. Mirages were quite the thing. You may note, as evidence, the Mirage Café at the second traffic lights after the police station in Child's Hill. The Mirage Bicycle Shop on Prince Albert Road. Hampstead's Mirage Billiard Parlour. Mirage Bakery. Mirage Haberdasher's. Mirage Mansions (a block of flats). Mirage Massage. These all received their name during that summer of the Mirage, and testify to its fame.

But in February of 1934, quietly, without much fanfare, the creation was demolished and replaced by a cinema – a branch of the Ionic chain – for, let's face it, who would wish to visit the Artificial Mirage more than once; and how boring to view an illusory fragment of one's own city when one could instead see *Pépé Le Moko* or *Nanook* . . . the North African casbah . . . the snowy redoubts of the Arctic . . . There may have been some who regretted the change, who preferred the subtle yet highly dramatic variations in the Mirage to Hollywood histrionics – but if so they were few, and drew no attention to themselves.

Curiously, once the Artificial Mirage had disappeared hardly anybody reported seeing the natural ones any more. Certain professors of optics, who took a professional interest in such matters, were puzzled: for there was every reason to suppose the climatic conditions which had given rise to the phenomenon in the first place were still operational; but they had more pressing business to attend to, or if they hadn't they felt they ought to have, and left it at that.

Nowadays, indeed, the mirages are seldom observed by natives of the city. Yet a refugee, not infrequently, will come across a detached floating luminous house or tree, and marvel. Or consider a child: who finds the simple apparition of imaginary water sufficient to excite the mind. Or a pair of lovers, strolling along the top of Parliament Hill, not long before sunset one afternoon in late summer. Side by side, they will stand on their heads, the better to view the inverted miniaturized fragment of the inner city. They will suppose the mirage has never existed before: that it has come into being just for them: that they are the ones, the only ones, for whom it was meant.

Xenolith

It is a city which decays. Not fast, not in some showy catastrophe, but all the same everything is in the process of breaking down and falling apart. Or at least it gives that impression – much as mourners, the tradition-minded ones, while not going as far as wearing sackcloth and ashes, rip their clothes along non-vital lapel-seams or dress in solid black, to imply, rather than demonstrate, grief. Off-white paint on the neoclassical exterior of the British Museum (storehouse of an ageing Empire's loot) flakes and peels and disseminates. Inside, a Wonder Of The Ancient World has been dismantled and crated, ready to be banished to some far basement in the English Midlands. The last remains of Nineveh disappeared aeons ago. Already the Elgin Marbles (ripped off from Greece) are absent; it is safe to predict that the Roman department will be boxed away next. What is left are the relatively unimportant items, or those which exist in many versions. Upstairs and back, in the Egyptological section, lesser deities in far from mint condition are permitted to hang on; surplus mummies lie supine in their mummy cloths. An ancient game is on display behind glass; it was salvaged from a tomb where it had been buried near a king that he might while away the afterlife; it involves a stone board engraved with rows of dimpled depressions, and coloured pebbles that were moved about according to certain rules – rules that nobody knows any more; it is playable only in archaeologists' dreams. Nearby, a cracked statue of Osiris persists on a plinth; a faded yellow label explains: on the 17th Athyr, in the twenty-eighth year of his reign, Osiris 'the Good One' fell under the blows of the conspirators led by his wicked brother Seth; who thereafter chopped the corpse into fourteen fragments and sent each to a different temple, that Osiris might never be reconstituted – on the Humpty Dumpty principle.

Yet in truth this exemplifies no more nor less than a theorem in physics: the Second Law of Thermodynamics: entropy increases. (The First Law states that energy is conserved: something at least does not change. The Third Law declares it impossible ever to quite reach absolute zero – in the event that anybody should try – knowing what cannot be done is in itself an achievement.)

What was once plentiful has become rare: eggs.

Rationing is coming into effect; the era of the three-yolk omelette (but months ago!) seems mythical. In Berwick Street market a colonel in an armoured (cavalry, historically) division's elbow accidentally collides with a dozen on a stall and knocks one off. It is only slightly crazed. With the aid of his brother officers plus their batmen, he attempts to make amends: the army crouches and examines and attempts to push the liquid contents back inside the jigsaw-puzzled shell – hopeless.

Yet there is another version of the Osiris story. Or call it a sequel – a to-be-continued. His loving widow, Isis, collected all his parts (you can see her in action on a bas-relief in The Doktor's study) or almost all (let us not speak of the incident of the severed phallus and the shellfish) and recomposed them, as Frankenstein his monster. Of course the resultant Osiris was not quite the same as the original; superior, arguably; a king had become a god.

And this is the positive side of entropy. By means of decay, change and growth is possible. Think of the most implausible turn of events: that an old, fat, cigar-chomping political has-been stands a chance of becoming Prime Minister; that (oh, dream away!) London Bridge should fall down yet be put back together again beside a lake in Arizona; that (insert the wish of your choice) . . . none of these, within reason, can be ruled out.

And the more that a dying or dead Doktor is attacked; the more he is decried and dismissed, even misunderstood; the more he is divided up and scattered and parts of him are venerated severally; despite that: by virtue of that, the more he lives.

Yacht

On the Serpentine in Hyde Park, in a small boat shaped like a teapot, Jones is afloat. He is dressed, out of respect, in a sombre suit and bowler. His boat, like all the boats on the lake, is a pedal-operated tandem. Unlike a bicycle built for two – in which one person takes the lead and controls the handlebars while the other simply follows and supplies extra energy – these boats are designed for a couple to sit side by side, close and reasonably equal. But Jones is on his own.

He is by no means the only solitary boatsman. When he had arrived at the queue at the rental booth near the bridge, he had imagined he would be trailing after a procession of romantic couples (or of children? no, it is no longer high summer: this is a weekday during term: there shall be no children) yet in fact singletons seem as common as pairs. Ah, this is an era when so many are bereaved: the wife is left behind while her husband is called up; the father waves goodbye to his evacuated boys; and (though they call this the Phoney War, and nobody is supposed to have really died as yet) individual deaths have occurred. He could have opted for a simple one-man rowing boat, an economy at one-and-eleven-three the hour, but he (like all the clientele) plonked down his half-crown and demanded a swanky tandem notwithstanding. As for the couples, Jones, as he signed the registration book, could not help but notice that the most common signature was 'Mr and Mrs John Smith' closely followed by 'Jones'.

The late afternoon sun, percolating through the foliage of beech trees and elms, burnishes the water. Over the lake of molten gold the teapot circulates, drifting at a cautious distance from other boats designed to resemble a goose, a carp, a fire engine, a banana . . . there is even one boat, surprisingly, which is made up in the likeness of a grandiose sailing boat, a yacht of sorts. Jones listens to the breeze and the water noise, and to the silence which is and for him always will be the silence of The Doktor. So Jones is analysed; but he has undergone analysis often: he presumes there is little more for him to learn about himself. He recognizes his more or less rational feelings of guilt; of triumph; of affection; of inchoate terror lest he should be found out; of relief indeed; and above all (though objectively he lives and works among friends and family: it is with difficulty that he has managed to secure this time for himself: he is far from alone) loneliness. This emotion is his now: it has been bequeathed to him.

Also he has inherited a selection of The Doktor's books, mostly those in English. And he has been given access to the papers so that he can complete the biography. He can make of the life what he will. Naturally he has no intention of dissimulating, of presenting any untruths, no not exactly, no hardly at all, no only when absolutely necessary – but being British he is skilled at the art of shading, adding and subtracting emphasis (for instance that flirtation The Doktor had once with the concept of Thanatos – the theory that a death instinct, vying with a love instinct, is at the bottom of all human passions – that will have to be downplayed, reduced to a bare allusive parenthesis or two), white-lying. And this is entirely proper; how absurd it would be to accuse the author of fictionalizing – for the genius of The Doktor is precisely that he is open to so many interpretations – any book about him just has to be a fiction. Jones opens *King Lear*. It is an unspecial Tauchnitz edition, decently bound, clear print, fits in a greatcoat pocket, but not in any way ornamental, quite without 'side'. It had been The Doktor's. 'I thought the King had more affected the Duke of Albany than Cornwall,' so the play begins with the conversation of two courtiers. Why yes, Jones is fondly reminded of the gossip at Psychoanalytical Congresses. He reads in silence, while pedalling his boat in a steady iambic pentameter, and keeping an eye out beneath his level bowler.

His attention wanders. He takes note of his fellow boaters. The loners certainly; the clown-faced spinster steering her apple; the man in Canadian Air Force uniform floating along in his motorcar; the speeding sheep propelled by a determined vicar . . . But also the couples, most of whom are scarcely bothering to pedal, letting the wind and waves take them where they may. Typically the man has his head buried in the woman's bosom, and she is gazing out over his shoulder in the direction of, as chance might have it, Jones. He stares back. Sometimes what he sees in her face is love or desire; though this is rare; and it pleases him. Sometimes a kind of greed. But all too often, and this is the norm, her expression is blank: she is thinking of (as far as Jones can tell) nothing. A colder wind skips across the Serpentine.

He returns to Shakespeare. There is much talk of dividing the kingdom. Lear himself appears, and as Jones reads the lines and hears them in his head, he envisions the King with his wisdom and pain and grey beard and glee and his air of unquestionable authority and his Viennese accent. (In Jones's imagination the beard is grander than ever The

Doktor's was, and the voice possesses a counterfactual Yiddish intonation.) Regan and Goneril sweet-talk the old man, though they mean to destroy him. Ah, it's the old story . . .

He breaks off in mid soliloquy – and steers the boat sharp right – for another vessel, in the form of a gingerbread cottage, is in danger of bearing down on his teapot. 'I say,' he calls out gently yet metrically, 'I say. I say. I say. I say.' The couple occupying the cottage jeers back; the male raises his fingers in a variant on what will, a few years later in the War, come to express V-for-Victory. The signer is evidently a policeman; his companion, judging by her clothing and make-up, a prostitute. Jones pedals parallel to them for some distance, neither closing in nor separating himself, in an exquisitely non-judgmental manner.

He can see them only above the waist, but some unbuttoning appears to be going on. No doubt she was paid in advance and, hungry, purchased a portion of fish and chips wrapped in a *Daily Mail*; judging by the aroma wafting over the Serpentine, she flavoured it with plenty of malt vinegar. She is more or less on top of her client. Jones thinks of her as divided like a centaur or mermaid: while her lower portion is carrying out its professional role, the upper part of her is engaged in eating the repast. Little can be seen of the man; from time to time, his helmet bobs up rhythmically.

Cordelia has her turn. Lear asks her, 'What can you say to draw a third more opulent than your sisters?' She responds, 'Nothing, my Lord.' Sometimes, however, a minimal response is not the most effective approach. 'Nothing!' 'Nothing.' 'Nothing will come of nothing, speak again!' And she delivers a long speech saying why she cannot say anything . . . betraying him, causing him to betray her. Well, she has no choice. The King will rage, and go mad, and die of heartbreak; and she will be responsible, in a way.

A tragedy, indeed. (Jones's hour is over; the controller calls to him through a megaphone, 'Come in, teapot! Your time is up!' Dutifully he pedals back to the shore.) But not simply that. It is also magnificent. And were the King not loved, and flattered by his enemies, and refused by the one who loves him, and misunderstood and understood too well, and killed, in private and in public, in print and on stage night after night, he would not be alive forever.

Zebra

On 1 January 1900, The Doktor wrote in his journal (which has been preserved, of course, among all his other documents and relics) 'The one thing I know about the coming century is that it contains the date of my death.'

And recurrently in the course of the following decades, in dark hours, unable to sleep, when another man might try to count sheep or compose a sexual fantasy, The Doktor calms himself by imagining the unimaginable: the world after he has left it.

It is the spring of one of those years near the beginning of the twenty-first century. London is transformed. From every direction of the compass, queues of patient tourists are tramping into the city. The phalanx of Americans, for instance, it stretches – by way of Finchley Road, Rosemont Road, Dresden Close, and so on across the suburbs of

Kilburn, Cricklewood, Willesden, Neasden . . . – westwards. The Europeans are coming from the east, arriving across Hampstead Heath and Highgate . . . From the north, via Hendon, descend the Scandinavian hordes . . . Africans are infiltrating up Baker Street . . . And all the lines converge on a detached house at number 20 Maresfield Gardens, once the residence of the Great Analyst himself, and now a museum dedicated to his memory. And who, knowing what we know, would not wish to visit, at least once in a lifetime, such a place?

For it has been established, beyond any question, that The Doktor was Right. Not just in outline, not that he asked relevant questions or broached new fields of inquiry, not that he was 'poetically' acute, no – every single thing he wrote, on every matter related to the mystery of human psychology, was the truth and the whole truth. Nothing more needs to be said. Now at long last we possess a complete understanding of consciousness.

The queues move slowly. Yet they move. To pass the time, the visitors crack their knuckles; they do amusing things with their eyebrows; they yawn; they knit; they carry out their voice exercises ('Mee ma mo ma mu,' they say, to train the lips and tongue; 'Nee na no na nu'); they bite open fortune cookies and swallow the fortune; they take out pocket chess sets (for preference, the magnetic kind that snaps open and shut like a crocodile's jaws) so as to play with themselves; they read – a botany textbook: they peer at the fine illustrations protected with tissue paper, or they might browse through a doctor-and-nurse, or a thriller; toddlers make up stories possessing remarkable coherence and narrative thrust on the basis of an illustrated alphabet book: the kind that begins with *apple* and ends with *zebra*. Food stalls cater to the visitors, offering fish and chips, fruit, a selection of gourmet buns, beer, sherry trifle. Musicians work the crowds: plus sword-swallowers, conjurors, creatures in zebra costumes juggling apples, creatures in apple costumes juggling zebras, and so forth. Also a less savoury element is present: it is not unknown for the grandfatherly character waiting patiently behind you to take out a pack of cards and suggest playing a game called poker; whereupon another stranger, a pretty woman perhaps, will offer to join in though she has never played it before, and she wonders if it might not be a good idea to bet a few pence a point, or cents, or yen, or euro . . . just to make it interesting. Yet it is wise to rein in excessive mistrust; on occasion a man and a woman will strike up a conversation, about the weather for instance, or the role of the Superego, or politics, and they will discover they share a sense of humour and find one another beautiful, and they will keep on talking.

The queues move surprisingly briskly, considering.

During opening hours (9–5, Monday to Saturday), for payment of a small entrance charge, it is permitted to visit the ground floor of number 20; also to peer down into the coal cellar and to climb up half a flight of stairs. One is encouraged to inspect the looking glasses. One may examine the portrait of him by Salvador Dali, a lock of his hair, his death mask. One may even (provided one's application has been previously approved) browse in the library of works on the subject of him and his. It is of course forbidden to enter the cordoned-off consulting room, yet – while the security guard has his back turned, chiding a teenager for spitting out a wad of blueberry-cheesecake-flavour gum on the fringes of the Persian carpet, say – it is not unknown for an eager visitor to scamper across, repose on the couch and pretend The Doktor himself is standing in silence at the head of it, then to dash back to the far side of the rope before the guard has had time to swivel around again.

More knowledge is to be had. Guide the cursor across the computer screen at the Museum Information Centre, click and double-click. Provided the question is among the Frequently Asked Questions, listed in alphabetical order, the answer shall be supplied.

Soon the visitor must leave, however, so that others will have a chance to enter. He or she is encouraged to write a parting comment in the Visitors' Book – 'Most interesting', or, 'I really appreciated it', or 'Wow!' . . . longer, more personal remarks are not considered appropriate. And then the visitor is outside again, on the street. In principle there is no reason why one should not return, but since, to do so, one would have to go all the way to the end of a queue, few if any ever actually will. All one has to show for the trip is, typically, a handful of postcards, a paperback of *Jokes And Their Relation To The Unconscious*, and a memory. Yet some have been granted more than that . . . a man from Uppsala and a woman from Ahmedabad, say: they will determine not to separate: they will make a new joint life for themselves in Newcastle-upon-Tyne. This kind of thing happens: it is possible, yet not very likely.

Ah, it is not easy, in this post-Doktor world. Ever since true understanding has been attained, it is no longer possible to dissemble emotions by means of some glib expression. One cannot say, referring to a mistake, 'Oh, it was just a slip of the tongue. It just popped out,' (for there are no slips which are just slips – nothing pops but it is pushed). Nor is it permissible, when speaking of the mutual attraction between two individuals, to declare: 'It's something chemical.' Or: 'They were meant for each other.' The strictly orthodox, indeed, will never say, 'I love you.'

Strangely, although all agree that The Doktor was correct about everything, it is not exactly clear what he intended.

His writings are pored over and interpreted; his analyses are re-analysed. It is argued that his later ideas are conclusive refutations of his earlier ones; it is argued that he was right when younger and went on to betray himself; it is argued that the truth in his works is diametrically opposed to what he thought he was saying. Criticism recurrently elevates him, if only to bring him down again. No matter: to know, as we do, that perfect knowledge of our own psyches is attainable, or that somebody once thought it was attainable, in principle, even: that alone is sufficient, and marvellous, and terrible.

The many, the very many, eager fans arrowing in to 20 Maresfield Gardens, we suppose they are pilgrims come to pay homage to a shrine – which they are, but what they also are, oh what we also are, is a mob, converging to destroy it.

S unlight infiltrates through a gap in the clouds, revealing the houses, their dark green or dark red roofs, the lightning conductors, the chimneypots arranged in rows like organ pipes, or separately like the various items on a tea tray . . . The sky shifts and the sun cuts out.

The suburb is hardly disturbed. It could pass for peaceable enough. A team of middle-aged Central Europeans is working its way along Fitzjohn's Avenue. The local council employs the refugees as painters: their job is to whitewash the base of the trees – pollarded planes, mostly – so that no one will crash into a trunk during the blackout. They take a noon break (tongue sandwiches) at the corner of Nutley Terrace; meanwhile a brush is borrowed and an amorous graffito appears on the bole of a horse chestnut. After lunch a refugee overpaints the motto in a swish of opaque white.

At number 11 Nutley Terrace old Mr S— is blowing 'No Name'

smoke – said to be efficacious against aphids – at his wilted rose-bush.

Mrs W— is affixing adhesive tape in a star pattern onto the bay window of number 17, an anti-shatter measure, just in case.

A sharp wind projects a back edition of *The Illustrated London News* along the pavement. The magazine twitches and leaps from stone to stone, hopscotching, flapping pages of political news, fashion, sport, court news; a cartoon poking fun at rumour-mongers; advertisements for officers' suitings, for stylish identity discs in silver or even platinum; table of contents; debutante of the month; index . . . It turns the corner into Maresfield Gardens (just as the sun comes out) and rolls over and over across the dusty road – a burning man trying to put himself out.

And when the sun has gone again, the magazine is invisible, recessed among mounds of blown-down leaves and general litter.

A man in an official capacity cycles past. He is wearing a safety helmet and a cape; also a notice is attached to the frame of his Raleigh three-speed: TAKE COVER. This is his duty, in the event of an air-raid warning. As a matter of fact there is no such danger: he is transporting the sign from place to place. In order to minimize the chance of confusing the public, he has fastened it upside down. Elsewhere no doubt, and at other times, it would be prudent to obey its message – but here, now, there is nothing that needs to be done.

There is not very much that needs to be done. A van has drawn up outside number 20. Its rear is open. Two men – one darker and one lighter – are emerging. They are, indeed, removal men of a sort.

They walk up the crazy-paved path, through the garden.

The blackout curtains are half-drawn across this house's windows.

They enter using the master key (which had been left for their benefit under a loose brick); not forgetting to wipe their boots on the Welcome mat.

Just within, as if standing sentinel, behold a combination coat-stand hat-stand umbrella-stand, an object of horned mahogany, currently coatless, hatless, umbrellaless. It is rather to one side, cornered; no need to move it: it will not get in the way.

And so into the room.

Dim. Quiet. A fine and private place. A secretaire, a side-board, a Middle Kingdom reliquary for a mummified falcon, cigar box, krater speckled with ash . . .

The darker man turns to face the lighter man.

A bronze of Isis suckling Horus is facing a framed photograph of a father and sons all in matching Alpine hats and leather shorts.

A love seat is facing a wastepaper basket.

The looking glasses are at either end of the couch, facing one another precisely.

The lighter man – a speck of dust has entered his nostril so he is on the point of sneezing but cannot altogether; if only it were sunnier: ah, if only there were more light, more light . . . 'Atishoo,' he declares, in three clear syllables, as if stating the word could bring on the instinctive action. His colleague blesses him, anyway.

The men are used to this business; to being alone and together in a strange place. They are used to silence. Silence is their element.

They take up their load. Between the two of them, the job is a reasonable one.

They exit with care, weaving their way between the various furnishings.

Lintel. Doorposts. Door knob.

Corridor.

Coat-stand.

(They glance around; as if they might have forgotten something; but there is no reason to suppose they have.)

Front door.

Welcome mat.

Narrow crazy-paved path through the garden (one man has to walk backwards all the time: the other man gets to go forwards) and past the gate, nudging it shut behind them; it clicks.

Outside, again.

In the distance, children sing as a rope is skipped over, and a dog barks, and a wireless'd politician rants, and these noises fade away to silence, or rather to near-silence for there is not nothing, no never.

A swallow leaves its nest by the roof guttering; circles the house once, and flies south.

The van is driven away, during a period of mild drizzle.

The drizzle patters on the windows of number 20; a breeze rattles the panes.

Then this too eases off.

Postscript

This novel is based on truth. Sigmund Freud did indeed, shortly before the War, flee to London, where he died of cancer. He was invited and accompanied there by his disciple and confidant, Dr Ernest Jones. The ideas attributed to Freud and to Jones can be found in their writings.

I have made some changes for the sake of crafting a novel. It was not in fact Jones but a certain Dr Schur who euthanased Freud. And whereas Freud's wife and daughter are only briefly alluded to in this novel, in reality they lived with him and cared for him in his last days.

But as for the fabulous city that Freud dreams up in this novel – I have lived there myself – its existence is not to be doubted.

*

Acknowledgements

I'd like to thank the Freud Museum in London, the Sigmund Freud Haus in Vienna; the Wellcome Institute for the History of Medicine; the British Library; the New York Public Library; the Bibliothèque Nationale, Paris; and the Hebrew University, Jerusalem. Also I'm grateful for comments and criticism from Dr Elizabeth Hollander and Dr Cheryce Kramer.